The Montana Rancher

The Montana Rancher

A Grand, Montana Romance

Paula Altenburg

TULE
PUBLISHING

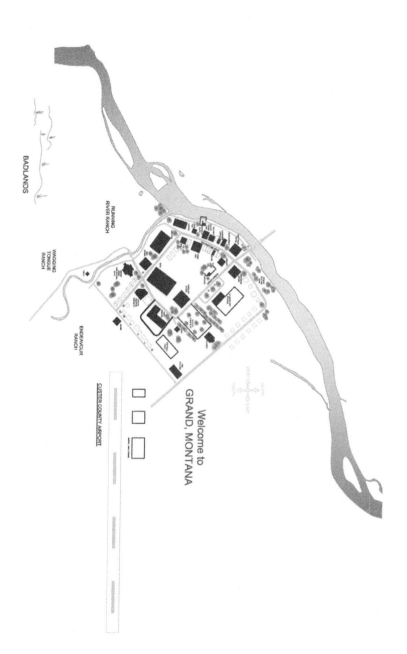

Welcome to
GRAND, MONTANA

BADLANDS

RUNNING
RIVER RANCH

WAGGING
TONGUE
RANCH

ENDEAVOUR
RANCH

CUSTER COUNTY AIRPORT

Chapter One

Elizabeth

ELIZABETH BENSON RANG the front bell of the Endeavour Ranch's main house. No one answered.

Flecks of ice stung her cheeks. She shrugged deeper into her fleece-lined coat and contemplated her next move—getting out of the wind. As a Chicago-born native, she was no stranger to raw, rainy weather, but late March in Montana on a cold, blustery day certainly gave her hometown a run for its money.

She'd been treated like royalty the moment she'd entered the FBO executive lounge at Chicago O'Hare International Airport. The private plane had been a nice touch. From Billings-Logan International, she'd transferred to a charter flight that had flown her to the small Custer County airfield outside of Grand, Montana, where a cab had been waiting for her.

Then the cab driver abandoned her here, in the middle of nowhere, with the sky's low-hanging, gray belly due to explode any second.

"There's always someone about," he'd cheerfully informed her while waving away her attempt to give him a tip. "No need for that. Bill's been paid."

She rang the doorbell again, leaning a little heavier on it this time. Still nothing, which didn't make sense. Why go to all the expense and trouble of flying her from Chicago to Montana for a job interview, then not be here to greet her?

She tried the door, which was unlocked, and peered inside. Calling this Goliath a house was like calling the Grand Canyon a crevice. An enormous lounge with a high-beamed ceiling and stone floor unfolded before her. Other than heavy leather furniture and a big-screen TV, it was empty and silent. On the other side of the lounge was an office. The door was open and the lights were off. Also empty. Since the lounge space appeared communal, not private, she dragged her suitcase inside. No one responded when she called out.

Her bootheels echoed off stone as she crossed the room to one of three imposing doors. A brass panel on the first door read, DAN MCKILLOP. Since Dan was the person who'd arranged for her interview, she rang the bell next to the brass panel. No answer. Of course there wasn't. She rang the next bell. DALLAS TUCKER. No one here either. She was beginning to feel a lot like Goldilocks. The third door belonged to Ryan O'Connell, the man she was here to see. No one home here, either.

The lounge area had a public restroom, so that took care of her most pressing concern. When she emerged, she debated curling up in one of the leather armchairs for a nap and completing the whole fairy-tale image. Eventually, someone would find her. This was a working ranch, after all, and while she didn't know much about ranching, she did know that the odd assortment of outbuildings she'd seen as she'd driven up the long drive in the cab had to support some sort of labor.

Therefore, discounting an apocalypse, the entire ranch couldn't possibly be deserted at three-fifteen in the afternoon. The cab driver hadn't thought so either, but since he'd been prepaid and there was no reason to put himself out, his opinion was suspect.

She tucked her bags out of sight between two leather chairs—she didn't care how deserted the place seemed—and again braved the fierce, icy wind raging outside that suggested the aforementioned apocalypse should not be ruled out. Chicago weather had nothing on this.

She covered her face with the sleek suede sleeve of her jacket and leaned into the wind as she battled her way to the first outbuilding. Inside, the shed smelled of grease, oil, and rust. Two boys, who had to be junior high students, not cowhands, glanced up as she entered.

"I'm looking for Ryan O'Connell," she said.

"He's in the calving shed, next to the heifer pen," one boy replied. He pointed to his right. Both boys went back to their task, which appeared to be tearing an engine apart, letting her know they'd given her all the directions she was likely to need.

Armed with this new information, Elizabeth backed out of the shed and into a flurry of wet, giant-flaked snow that clung to her eyelashes and melted upon contact with her cheeks. She'd heard blizzards weren't rare in the spring. It seemed the rumors were true.

And a heifer was some sort of cow, right?

She scanned the yard. To her left—in the direction the boy indicated—she spied a cluster of brown and black humps coated in white, bunched up to a fence, their skinny tails to the wind. A sloped shed with more of the ubiquitous steel siding butted the enclosure. She leaned into the wind and fought her way to the door of the shed. The slickened, muddy ground turned to ice under her feet and she slipped as she forced the sliding door open, saved from tumbling to her knees by her grip on the vertical handle.

"Close the damn door!" someone barked.

She regained her footing along with her composure and did as commanded. The warm interior of the calf shed was a welcome respite from the storm despite the frigid tone of its occupant. A barrage of foreign invaders attacked the inside of her nose. The scent of sweet-smelling hay mingled with urine and dust. The tang of manure with an overlay of coppery blood. Antiseptic—which quite frankly, was wasting its time.

A bright, overhead bulb spotlighted the scene. A dark-haired man crouched on his heels at the back end of a prone cow, one arm wedged well up under her tail, while the cow moaned her opinion in unhappy terms. Since he was the only person here, he had to be Ryan O'Connell. Her first impression of him was of dark, single-focused intensity wrapped up in excrement-splattered, heavy, blue-cotton coveralls.

He withdrew his arm, covered in a long, clear plastic glove that extended to his armpit, as well as a thick coating of stuff she didn't dare dwell on. The two tiny hooves in his hand explained a few things—number one being what the term calving shed meant.

Before she could recover her speech, he barked out another command without turning around. "Don't stand there. Make yourself useful. Hand me that chain on the wall." He jabbed an elbow behind him and held out his palm, jerking his fingers in a come-hither motion with all the patience of a Catholic school nun after a wad of contraband chewing gum.

She hoped he didn't plan on shouting at at-risk teenagers this way or they were going to have words.

A length of linked steel chain with two triangular handles on either end hung from a hook. She lifted the chain gingerly, questioning what some of the crusty stains on it might be, and dropped it into his waiting hand.

He stripped off the glove and tossed it aside, wrapped the chain around the two dangling front legs, grasped the handles in both hands, planted a rubber boot against the cow's nether end, and leaned back, tugging hard. His face reddened with strain as the cow's displeasure increased.

Seconds later, a small, wet body slithered free to land on a padding of thick yellow straw. The man flipped the limp calf over, wiped it down with his bare hands, then cleared its nostrils to make sure it was breathing.

The cow, like any new mama, immediately forgot her recent distress and got in a few licks with her tongue as she explored the world's newest member. The calf struggled to its knees, its efforts to rise hampered by its mother's effusive attention.

"That was incredible," Elizabeth breathed, unable to hold back her wonder at the miracle she'd witnessed.

The man glanced around. Surprise livened his face, stripping off years. He was a lot younger than she'd thought. And obviously, she wasn't who he'd expected to find standing behind him.

"Elizabeth Benson," she added, holding out her hand before thinking better of it and hastily jamming it into her jacket pocket. His look of confusion persisted, so she prodded his memory. "If you're Ryan O'Connell, I had a job interview scheduled with you for this afternoon?"

Ryan

NEVER AGAIN WOULD Ryan let Dan McKillop vet resumes for him. He'd told him three times that this particular candidate wouldn't suit, and yet, here she was—in the calving shed, of all places.

Amber-eyed Elizabeth Benson, with curly strands of fiery red hair escaping the hood of a form-fitting, camel suede jacket, and sporting a pair of black, knee-high leather boots drawn over black spandex leggings, looked like the tooth fairy's super-hot sister. The online footage of her didn't come close to the real thing. She had a perky, uptilted nose and full, pink-tinted lips. Her smooth, milk-white skin was unmarred by wrinkles, freckles, or anything so crass as a pimple. Long eyelashes had been dipped in milk chocolate, leaving them brown at the tips and dark red near the roots. The form her suede jacket fitted was fine. Very fine.

Too fine. What the hell had been going on in Dan's head?

They couldn't have this girl living on-site as a case manager for a group of delinquent teenaged boys. She was a walking, talking, wet dream. Hiring her would be asking—no, pleading—for trouble.

"Was your interview this afternoon?" he said, stalling, even though it made him sound disorganized and stupid, which he wasn't, but he couldn't very well tell her that he hadn't intended to interview her.

"According to the travel arrangements." *Which you made* her tone added.

But he hadn't. Dan had.

He cursed his friend. Crap, amniotic fluid, urine, and

blood covered his clothes and his hands. Likely his hair, too. The odds suggested his smell might not be daisy fresh, either. He'd ended up on birthing duty this afternoon because the night manager was off for another three hours and the two stooges in the machine shed had sissied out. They'd noted the heifer, a first-timer, was taking too long to deliver, brought her into the calving shed, then hauled him out of his office to come take a look. He cursed them out too.

Fortunately, the heifer showed the makings of a good mother. He lifted the calf—also a heifer—to its feet and helped it find one of the business ends of the udder. Once he had it latched on and was sure the mother's milk had let down, he returned his attention to Elizabeth. He hated to tell her she'd come here for nothing, but better to yank that particular Band-Aid off quickly.

He straightened. She was even prettier up close. And, given the length of her legs, a lot shorter than she'd appeared when he'd been crouched on his heels, looking up. The top of her head maxed out at the middle of his chest and she had to tilt her chin to look him in the eye.

"I'm sorry, Ms. Benson, but—" he began, only to get cut off before he could finish.

"Elizabeth."

He had an unholy urge to see how she'd react if he called her Beth. Or maybe Betty. Neither of which would suit her. Everything about her, from her overall appearance to her work experience, screamed money and privilege. Even her name. The Endeavour was no place for her.

"Elizabeth," he amended. "I apologize for not being better prepared, but this is how life goes on a ranch. There's a storm rolling in, meaning all available hands are out on the range, feeding cattle and gathering up any babies they think might not survive the weather." He began to feel like a jerk for making it sound as if she didn't matter. She was a human being, not a farm animal. "Come on up to the house. You can have a coffee while I take a quick shower. Then I'll run you into town before the storm settles in. You'll spend the night at the Yellowstone Hotel." He didn't know what arrangements Dan had made for her and couldn't very well ask. He did know that planes weren't going to fly. Neither were pigs.

If she'd noticed he said nothing about the actual interview, she didn't let on. Ms. Elizabeth Benson didn't appear to be the type of woman to waste words, a definite point in her favor, if there could be such a thing.

He ducked into the operating room where C-sections were performed to wash his hands so he didn't spread bacteria over every surface he touched. Then, beckoning for her to follow, he slid the steel outer door back on its tracks. It stuck, meaning the temperature had dipped below freezing, and he leaned in to work it free. A blast of un-March-like winter struck him full in the face and bit through the heavy weave of his damp coveralls. Two inches of snow had buried the ground while he was delivering the calf. Montana did nothing halfway.

The wind caught Elizabeth, who likely weighed a hundred pounds at the most, and he seized her arm to keep her from blowing away. He reevaluated his plan. Common sense said driving her into town in these conditions would be stupid, especially when they had plenty of empty rooms at the house. Or she could stay in the bunkhouse they'd set up for permanent staff if she didn't like the thought of sleeping at the main house with three strangers—although Dallas, a doctor, and Dan, the county sheriff, would likely stay in Grand for the night rather than tackle the roads in a blizzard.

He brightened. Having her spend the night at the ranch was the better solution, at that. She'd get to see how isolated they were. There were no other women within a twenty-mile radius.

They stumbled through the storm, although headway was slow. Ryan did his best to keep the brunt of the wind, snow, and sleet off Elizabeth, who struggled behind him. Finally, they entered the house through a side door that led directly into a mudroom off his private apartment. The mudroom had a shower attached for these types of situations.

He brushed the snow off as best he could, then kicked off his boots and began to unzip his coverall. Elizabeth remained on the mat in front of the door, dripping water and looking uncertain. Since he wore jeans and a flannel shirt underneath his coverall, meaning he wasn't stripping down naked, he didn't know what that look was about.

"Where do I leave my boots and coat?" she asked.

Oh.

"Hang your coat on that hook and you can leave your boots on, if you like," he replied.

"My feet are wet." Delicate eyebrows rose a half inch as she pointed out something that probably should have been obvious. Those knee-high leather dress boots might be sexy as hell, but practical, they weren't.

He cast around for a solution. "Here." He scrabbled through the contents of a shelf in the closet and withdrew a pair of thick wool socks for her and a stack of clean clothes for himself. He passed her the socks. "Put your boots by the heater. You can wear these while they dry. The kitchen's through there. The coffeemaker's on the counter—it's press and go. The pods are beside it and the cream is in the fridge. Help yourself to whatever you like in the cupboards." He gestured to the tiny bathroom and shower. "I'll be a few minutes."

She peeled off her coat and hung it to dry. Underneath, she wore a black tunic with a flared skirt over the black leggings. A funky checkered gray scarf topped her ensemble. None of it hid her curves. A mass of cherry-red, spiral curls played with her shoulders. The cute nose and delicate skin glowed faintly pink from the cold. Again, he was struck by how pretty she was.

Removing the wet leather boots proved to be a bit of a struggle for her. He itched to help out as she balanced on one foot, but the offer might come across as too bold, so he left her to it and ducked into the bathroom where he could breathe. That hot little babe around a bunch of hormone-addled boys?

So not going to happen.

A short while later, he strolled into the L-shaped kitchen.

This was his favorite room in the whole house and where he spent most of his free time. The island was square, with a vegetable prep sink in the middle, built for entertaining. The counters and cupboards, the main sink, and the industrial-grade appliances, were all within easy reach. Along the bottom part of the L, he'd installed a round kitchen table, a sofa and chairs, and a fireplace with a seventy-two-inch flat-screen TV mounted above it. He counted on Dan and Dallas to produce a dozen or so offspring apiece so he could host parties in here. They might not be brothers for real, but they were like brothers to him, and he planned to be the overin-dulgent uncle who spoiled their kids rotten.

She'd perched on one of the barstools at the granite is-land and was sipping a cup of coffee, looking as if she belonged here. For some reason that bugged him. The socks he'd loaned her reminded him of those floppy-toed shoes the men wore in the Middle Ages. Her feet had to be inside them somewhere, but where, was anyone's guess. She'd rolled them down several times and they bulged at her ankles.

He caught a whiff of her coffee. She'd chosen the caramel flavor, his favorite, so he did the same. He pushed the button on the coffeemaker, and thirty seconds later, his drink was ready. He straddled a stool and eyed his companion. Yup. She was much, much too pretty.

The storm had picked up steam, too. Nothing visible but a sheet of white on the other side of the windows.

"So, Elizabeth," he said, sipping his drink. The shower had gone a long way toward heating him up and the hot coffee sliding into his belly finished the job. "That trip into town's not looking good at the moment." He held out hope that the storm would let up before dark. If it turned back to rain, the snow would melt fast. It was March, after all. It could happen. "We might as well get your interview out of the way while we wait for things to improve. Your resume is a little light on detail." She'd earned a master's degree in social work at an impressive college, and she had the hours in for her license, but her direct work experience was lacking. He had no idea why Dan thought she was such a great candidate to work with troubled teenaged boys. "Tell me a bit about yourself and why you'd like to work at the Endeavour's group home." *Convince me.*

Amber eyes kicked the heat up a notch in his belly as she answered him with a question. "Can I assume you've seen news footage of me?"

"Yes."

He had, indeed. Elizabeth Benson was an outspoken advocate for victims' rights. She championed anyone who'd been impacted by violent crime. In the past year, she'd helped three families in the Chicago area who'd lost family members—one was a gang-related, drive-by shooting and two involved domestic murder-suicides. Rumor had it she'd lost a sister years ago in some sort of accident, but the details around it were murky. He'd done enough unproductive digging to figure out the Bensons kept a tight lid on their private business.

He knew all about keeping family business private. It made him curious as to whether or not the Chicago-based Bensons might have known Giaco Cienetti. They likely knew of him. Everyone did. *The insane bastard.*

He stomped memories of his deceased grandfather down where they belonged and got back to the matter at hand. Chicago was another strike against her. He didn't like the reminder of a place he preferred to forget. Where was she going with this?

"What I never talk about," Elizabeth continued, those clear, amber irises steady on him and her voice matter-of-fact, "is that my sister Marianne was murdered by her boyfriend when she was eighteen. I was eleven. My parents never recovered from it. They don't speak of it to this day and they don't talk about her. Ever. I first got into social work because I wanted to understand them. I thought maybe I could help them work through their anger and grief. But I also wanted to understand the mindset of Marianne's killer. Why did he do it? What led him to believe that murder was the right course of action? He came from a good home. Or it seemed that way from the outside looking in. That's why I want this job. I want to learn as much as I can about the way troubled boys think in order to help stop the violence before it begins. Marianne wasn't the only victim. My parents were too, but so was her murderer. His parents, his teachers, and his friends all either missed or ignored the warning signals, because there had to be something. My research while I'm here will go toward my PhD dissertation."

The only break in the silence was the clatter of ice pellets striking the windows. The power flickered, then held. If it lost its grip, the generator would kick in.

"*Great*," Ryan thought. "*Now how am I supposed to tell her she can't have the job?*"

Chapter Two

Ryan

RYAN BARRICADED HIMSELF in his office, scuffed stacks of notes aside, and called Dan on the landline. Since Dan had arranged for the interview with Elizabeth, despite repeatedly being told she wouldn't suit, he could be the one to give her the bad news.

"No way," Dan said. "I did due diligence, buddy. She's got her master's, her qualifying experience, and she's licensed to work in Montana as a registered clinical social worker. She specializes in addiction and wants to do research on teenaged violent offenders. She's the best case manager you're going to find."

"She's five feet tall," Ryan said. He was exaggerating, but not by a lot. She might be five two, maybe three at best. "And she's hot. Putting her in front of a group of hormonal boys is like waving a raw steak at a starving grizzly."

Dan's low chuckle crackled over the line. "My understanding is that her parents insisted she learn how to defend herself."

"That's another thing." Ryan felt the sweat begin to form at his hairline, followed by a familiar chill that chased through his chest. "You know why they'd insist on it, right? Her sister was murdered. That shit will mess with your head."

There was a slight pause on Dan's end, and immediately, Ryan regretted his words. He didn't like being psychoanalyzed and Dan knew it. And, as law enforcement, Dan was very good at picking up on the things people didn't say.

"Your goal is to help these boys. If you provide a safe work environment for the qualified professional hired to treat them, your job as an employer is done," Dan said. "She'll do her own risk assessments and decide which boys the ranch will take in."

Ryan leaped on what was important in Dan's less-than-motivational speech. "How the hell am I supposed to provide a safe work environment for her on a ranch?"

"Add extra lighting around her bunkhouse. Motion sensors would be good. Move her office into the space next to yours. Put in an intercom system so that if she's ever alone with one of the boys and feels threatened, all she has to do is flip a switch and whoever's working in the machine shed will get an alert. There's always someone around if she needs them. But honestly, my take on Elizabeth Benson is that she can look out for herself. I checked her references and they concurred. She's not a risk-taker. She's not easily intimidated either."

Didn't he know it. "Have a heart, Dan."

"Do you want what's best for these boys or are you trying to make things easy for you?" Dan countered, then mellowed his stance. "I get that you're trying your hardest to fulfill the terms of the inheritance while running the ranch, but you're taking on too much. You agreed I could find you a case manager and I did. A damned good one, too. The correct response in this situation is thank you."

So many layers of guilt bombarded Ryan. Dan and Dallas believed the judge who'd given them community service for stealing a police car back in college had left the Endeavour and several billion dollars to them, but with conditions attached. Dan had to provide emergency services, including smoke jumping, to the state of Montana. Dallas Tucker, a doctor, had to operate a free medical clinic. Ryan had agreed to set up and oversee a group home for troubled teenaged boys.

Only, those conditions for the inheritance were bogus. So was the source of the money. Ryan dreaded the day they found out what a liar he was. Correction. They'd known for years that he was a liar. What they didn't know was the extent of the most recent lie he'd concocted.

"Thanks, Dan. Thanks a whole lot."

Dan laughed. "I'm sorry you're stuck all alone in a blizzard with a gorgeous redhead, but the roads aren't fit to travel. I'm going to have to spend the night with my parents. Dallie's at the taproom with Hannah."

Hannah Brand owned the Grand Master Brewery and Taproom, a place where locals went to drink her craft beers and play board games. Dan's significant other, Jazz O'Reilly, ran the smoke jumping base at Custer County Airport for him. Jazz worked in Helena as a firefighter during the off season, which was where she was at the moment, but Ryan expected that situation to change as soon as she found something more permanent in Grand. The constant trips back and forth had to be killing them both.

"See you in the morning," Dan said, then hung up.

Ryan dropped the receiver into the cradle and rubbed his eyes. They'd lost power a half hour ago and it wasn't likely to be reinstated anytime soon. The outage meant Elizabeth would either have to sleep in the main house or the calving shed, the only other building on the ranch with a generator wired in.

He couldn't imagine her spending the night in a barn, no matter how unfazed she'd been when he'd hauled that calf free. But it gave him an idea.

By the time he returned to the kitchen, the pixie had nestled herself into a deep-cushioned chair in front of a bay window and was watching the storm. Snow blew past horizontally as if propelled by a giant, hidden fan. None of the outbuildings, mere yards from the house, could be seen through the thick wall of white.

"It's hard to believe it's March," Elizabeth said.

"Spring in Montana—the blip between winter and two

weeks of summer. After that we get a month of fall before the cycle repeats. If you like skiing and snowmobiling, this place is heaven."

"I like snow."

He did too, but he wasn't trying to sell it to her. Quite the opposite. "It's great if you don't have to go anywhere, but there's nothing within walking distance, so someone's always out running errands. There isn't much of an opportunity for a social life here, either."

"I have a car and I'm fine with running errands to help out," she said. "The unstructured lifestyle was part of the appeal of the position."

She was a social worker, all right. They had this perverse desire to present opposing and unusually perky opinions. Worst of all, she wasn't taking the hint.

"Speaking of helping out…" Ryan parked himself in the chair facing her. The small kitchen nook by the bay window was where he relaxed with his coffee and tablet to read the news after chores in the mornings. "Ranches run twenty-four seven. Everyone who lives here has to pull their own weight. Right now, we have a night manager in the calving shed because babies are dropping right, left, and center, but once calving season is over, he'll move on to another job for a few months. That doesn't mean calving stops. We get lots of them born out of season. Any the mothers won't accept will have to be bottle fed. That'll be your responsibility. You'll have a few foals, too. And there are always abandoned kittens around."

Elizabeth's eyes lit up with an enthusiasm he didn't like. "You'd allow me to bottle-feed babies?"

"Twenty-four seven," he reminded her, although he began to suspect he was fighting a battle he'd already lost. He took note of the time. "Since you're stuck here for the night anyway, why don't we go out right now and I'll show you what's involved?"

"In this storm?" She showed her first visible signs of doubt. Snow mixed with ice pellets pinged off the windows like excited atoms colliding with particles. He knew exactly how much they stung when they hit exposed skin.

"Calves don't wait for fair weather," he said, shooting out of his chair. "Come on. Livestock eats before we do."

She stood, but with less speed. Her enthusiasm didn't die but it dropped a few noticeable degrees. She indicated the pair of socks he'd loaned her that flopped about three inches past the tips of her toes. "I don't have the right clothes and my boots are wet."

"No worries. I can fix that."

He found a thick sweater of his that fit her about as well as the socks. The hem teased her knees and the shoulders drooped midway to her elbows. She had to roll the cuffs up into great, bulky bulges. Dan's nieces and nephews were frequent weekend guests, so he scrounged around in his space and came up with a coverall and rubber boots suitable for both ten-year-old boys and undersized women. He topped her outfit off with a tin cloth jacket that belonged to Dan's girlfriend, a wool scarf, and a knitted wool hat. The hat was to protect her hair from picking up barn smells as much as her head from the storm.

Amber eyes buried in wool glittered at him. "I feel like the Michelin Man."

He gave her appearance a quick, critical assessment. Man, she was tiny. He had a foot of height on her, although dressed as she was, if he measured her sideways, that was up for debate. Her arms stuck out to the sides. All to be seen of her face was her cute little nose, finely shaped brows, and those dark-lashed, amber eyes with the traces of yellow gold embracing the pupils. Not even the layer of mismatched, oversized barn clothes could disguise how pretty she was.

I hate you, Dan.

"If it helps, once you're covered in snow, you're going to look like the Michelin Man, too," he said.

The cute little nose crinkled at him. "Thank you."

He donned coveralls and boots, plus a hat and coat. "After you, Michelin," he said, ushering her ahead of him into the maelstrom with a sweep of his arm.

She waddled to the door. He sincerely hoped the wind didn't catch her again. He had visions of her tumbling across the yard, gathering snow like a giant snowball, and smacking into the barn.

If this didn't scare her off, nothing would.

Elizabeth

ELIZABETH HAD ASSUMED the job was hers. That all she had to do was show up and prove she was as qualified and capable as her curriculum vitae indicated. The Endeavour Ranch had paid to fly her here, after all.

Now, she wasn't so sure.

Ryan O'Connell wasn't what one would expect of a hands-on, billionaire philanthropist with a soft spot for troubled boys. In her head, she'd pictured someone more nurturing. A natural caretaker. Instead, he was darker. Broodier. A whole lot more Heathcliff from *Wuthering Heights* and less Mr. Rogers. The slight cleft in his chin gave him a baby-faced appeal, complicating him further. She couldn't figure out if he was a youthful ninety-year-old or an ancient thirty-something, but she had her suspicions.

She wasn't about to let Heathcliff find a reason not to give her this job, however, so she pulled up her panties—figuratively, not literally, because who could find them under all of these clothes—and plunged into the storm. Ice bit her cheeks and rendered her blind. Her arms pinwheeled wildly. For a second, she feared she might become airborne and imagined her body landing in Kansas once the storm dropped her.

Then Heathcliff—if she survived, she had to stop calling

him that—grabbed the back of her coat and helped keep her borrowed boots on the ground. "Better let me go first," he shouted over the howl of the wind. "Stay close behind me."

Easier for him to say. The ground in front of the door to the house had been swept almost bare, but two of the drifts between the house and the calving shed came to her waist. Twice, Ryan had to turn back and pull her free. The speed with which spring could flip back to winter left her in awe. Montana was truly amazing. It made a person appreciate how wonderful it was to be alive.

They reached the shed and Ryan leaned into the edge of the sliding door, heaving it open despite the buildup of snow. Elizabeth stumbled inside. The calving shed was reasonably warm, quiet, and calm, considering the weather raging outside. They brushed the snow off their coats.

A man in his fifties, with a thick crop of gray hair and a slight stoop to his shoulders, looked up from a pail of what had to be milk that he held under a calf's snuffling nose. The calf headbutted the sides of the steel pail, almost knocking it out of his hands. He propped the pail against one thigh and held it steady with a tight grip as he checked to see who had intruded.

"Hey, Freddie," Ryan called out in greeting. "Did the men all make it back from the pastures okay?"

"Yep. Young John got an ATV stuck in the mud near the badlands but managed to work himself free. He came in late, but not so late that we had to go looking for him. Steve and

Handy brought eight heifer calves and two bull calves in with them. Three newborns are under the heat lamps, thawing out." Freddie's eyes, spit-firing curiosity, lit on Elizabeth. "Who have we here?"

Ryan shucked his coat and slung it over a wooden rail fronting one of the pens. He fumbled behind Elizabeth for the ends of the ice-stiffened scarf protecting her face and began to unwrap her, as if peeling an orange. "This is Elizabeth. She's from Chicago. Elizabeth, meet Freddie Harrington. He's our night manager during calving season."

"Pleased to meet you," Elizabeth said. She stuck a glove under one of her arms and pried it off so she could shake hands, but Freddie, who'd set down the pail, held his own hands in the air, out of reach.

"You don't want to be touching what I've touched," he said, half apologetically, half smiling.

"She'll be touching it plenty if she takes the case manager's job," Ryan interrupted. "Feeding orphaned calves will be part of her duties."

"So… you brought her out in a blizzard to show her all the fun she'll miss out on if she turns the job down?" Freddie scratched his neck as if trying to figure out the logic behind it. "You should have let Dallas or Dan handle her interview for you, boss man. You forget how to hire women. You don't give them the bad news up front."

"I'm not hiring a woman—I'm hiring a case manager for a position that happens to be on a working ranch, where we all end up doing work outside of our formal job descriptions," Ryan said, with a touch too much smugness for Elizabeth's liking.

Her lips pressed together. Just as she suspected. Heathcliff really was trying to discourage her from accepting the position. She'd see about that.

She got her other glove off—calfskin might not have been her most sensitive choice, given the circumstances—and unzipped the front of the canvas coat he'd loaned her. "Gentlemen, part of the reason I applied for this position is precisely because it's on a ranch. I'm happy to feed orphaned calves, and any other orphaned babies who require it."

"There's the right attitude," Freddie congratulated her, his gray-stubbled face creased with a smile. "This one's big enough to be weaned"—he indicated the calf he'd been feeding from the pail—"but the three little ones under the heat lamp will need bottles. Let me get you started."

He grabbed a large plastic jug sitting in a bucket of warm water and poured a thick, yellow liquid into a baby bottle he'd taken from a cupboard next to the fridge, then screwed on a nipple as big as her thumb.

"This milk looks spoiled," she said, crinkling her nose doubtfully as he passed the bottle to her and began filling another.

"It's colostrum," Ryan explained. He'd been watching her as if this were some sort of test, which it unquestionably was. "We keep it on hand for the newborns. It contains natural antibodies. If they don't get it in the first few hours, most of them will sicken and die." Freddie passed a second bottle to him.

Minutes later, they each had a newborn calf under their care. Freddie showed her how to moisten her fingers with the warmed liquid and stick them in the calf's mouth. It took a few tries, but soon the calf began an instinctive suckling, its rough little tongue tickling her skin. By the time Freddie helped exchange the nipple for her fingers, she was in love with the soft, sweet-smelling, rusty-haired baby and entranced by its large brown eyes, which were half-closed in bliss.

When the calf finished feeding, she reluctantly allowed Freddie to return it to its place with its bunkmates under the heat lamp.

"What will happen to them?" she asked.

"We'll try to get them back with their mothers once the weather lets up," Freddie said. He checked the tags on their ears, an adornment she hadn't noticed. "These three have seasoned moms, not first-timers, so it shouldn't be too much of a problem. Sometimes the first-timers won't take them after they've been handled by us, and if another mother won't step up, we have to keep bottle-feeding them. That's what happened to this big girl, over here." He indicated the calf with the pail, now curled up and asleep in its pen.

"This is where you'll come in," Ryan said gruffly.

Elizabeth thrilled at his wording, although solid confirmation that the job really was hers would be nice, because he sounded far from excited. It didn't take a clairvoyant to figure out he wasn't happy to be bringing a woman on board, but if it was such a problem for him, why go to the trouble of flying her out here in the first place?

The two men talked for a bit, then she and Ryan bundled up and struck out for the house. The storm, barreling along like a runaway train, showed no signs of losing steam. She was relieved when they made it safely inside. They shucked their wet clothing and washed up. A quick check of the clock in the kitchen said the hour fast approached seven o'clock.

"I hope you're okay with bacon and biscuits," he said, reaching under a counter to extract an enormous black, cast-iron frying pan. He plunked it on top of an industrial gas range. "I wasn't expecting company for supper."

Elizabeth rested her toes on one rung of a stool at the island to keep from sliding off. It was either that or leave her feet dangling like a six-year-old child's. Then, she studied her potential employer.

He was a good-looking man. Or he could be, if he didn't come across as even more remote than his ranch. Physical labor gave him shoulders and a chest a bodybuilder would envy. She'd bet under that sweater lurked a decent six-pack, too. Brown hair—short on the sides and slightly longer on top, barely enough to give it a curl—and deep, dark, brown eyes added to the whole "loner" mystique.

Those endless eyes harbored secrets. She knew it. And it was in her nature to want to know what they were, but that wasn't what was important right now.

"I get the feeling you weren't expecting me at all," she said.

She'd decided directness was the best approach in this situation, but not too direct. It wouldn't do to put him on the defensive. Besides, Heathcliff would never admit that his reluctance involved her being a woman.

And while she wanted the job, a hostile work environment would hardly benefit either of them, not to mention the unhealthy spillover effect it would have on troubled teens. It wasn't as if he could avoid her. The Endeavour Ranch was the equivalent of a deserted island. The vast majority of the county's real estate belonged to the ranch, and at a whopping six thousand, the town of Grand housed half of the county's population. The entire state of Montana possessed only one-tenth that of Chicago.

He pulled a paper-wrapped packet of meat from the fridge and began laying cold slabs of Canadian bacon in the pan. Elizabeth didn't dare ask about vegetables—like maybe a salad—because she suspected the answer already.

"Dan McKillop arranged for your interview," he said. "What with one thing and another, and everyone so busy, we didn't get a chance to discuss any of the details. I guess it slipped both our minds."

She wondered how Dan had dared. She got the sense

Ryan didn't much care for surprises. He had control issues for sure. She recognized the flaw because she had it, too.

She didn't give up easily, either. "I'm aware of the pitfalls for a woman working with teenaged boys." That was the whole point of her study. "It also has its advantages, particularly since some boys have difficulty with male authority figures. I'm excited by the opportunity to get to do hands-on research for my dissertation and I'm happy to help around the ranch in any way I can. Since Montana has a mandatory six-month probationary period for new employees, why not give me a chance to prove my ability?"

The meat began to sizzle in the pan. The smell of maple and smoke made her empty stomach sit up and take notice. Ryan rummaged in a cupboard and found an enormous tin. He pried the lid off the tin and shook thick, golden-topped biscuits onto a plate. She could practically see the wheels in his head spinning as he tried to come up with an argument that would hold water, and isolated the exact moment he caved.

"Welcome to the Endeavour Ranch," he said. "Your six-month probation will begin at the first of the month."

A flicker of emotion stirred in his eyes. It might have been resignation. Annoyance was another distinct possibility. Whatever it was, she didn't care. The job was hers. Excitement victory-danced all over her hunger, trampling it into oblivion.

Now, to go home and break the news to her parents.

Chapter Three

Elizabeth

"RYAN O'CONNELL IS a man with no past," Theodore Benson announced in a dire tone heavy with prediction and doom, leaving Elizabeth to draw her own conclusions as to what he inferred.

She didn't respond straight away. Her athletic father, his blond hair scuffed with gray at the temples, could cut an imposing—some might go so far as to say intimidating—figure when he chose, even here, in the feminine surroundings of her bedroom.

Seated in one of the matching pink-and-white Queen Anne chairs tucked beneath the bay window, he exuded disapproval. He adjusted the creases of his trouser legs so they draped neatly and evenly over his knees. He could have been sitting in one of his board meetings, listening to a budget report that didn't match up to his high expectations.

She was a lot like that budget report to him, sometimes. Her parents had been appalled when she told them she'd accepted a job in Montana and horrified that she planned to drive her car eleven hundred miles alone.

She rolled a sweater and carefully packed it around several fragile items in her bulging suitcase to protect them. She was a little sad to leave Chicago, but also excited. She'd reviewed the profiles she'd been sent on the first ten boys the ranch would take in and they were an interesting mix. Two were violent offenders with extenuating circumstances. A third had been charged with sexual offenses against a minor, but the boy's probation officer was unconvinced he was guilty as charged.

More interesting, as far as her research was concerned, were the seven boys with no juvenile records who'd all been removed from family homes along with their younger siblings. Foster placement was difficult for their age group and each had begun to act out in what might well be cries for help. Two had vandalized their schools. One stole a car and was caught joyriding at one hundred miles per hour on the interstate. The remaining four had run away from group homes on multiple occasions. None of the seven had a history of substance abuse or addiction, which came as the biggest surprise.

Living in Montana would be an adventure all on its own. She'd been disappointed in Grand at first, mainly because the town was part of the prairies and she'd anticipated mountains, but there were badlands that begged to be explored and mountains not so far off. She'd read up on the Rocky Mountain Range, and the Beartooth Mountains were high on her list of places to explore on her days off. The thought of it left her almost giddy.

"And you know this how?" she asked, circling back to her father's big revelation, mostly because she was expected to say something and not because this was news to her.

She'd conducted her own research on the Endeavour Ranch's three owners, and while Sheriff Dan McKillop and Dr. Dallas Tucker were pretty much open books, Ryan was a complete and utter dead end. She'd found the story on how the three men were left the ranch, as well as an estimated four billion dollars, by an unnamed benefactor. She knew there were conditions attached to the inheritance, one of them being the group home for at-risk teenaged boys. She knew prior to that, Ryan had worked as an operations manager for an auction and rodeo house in Houston, Texas. And she knew he'd gone to Montana State University, where the three men met and became friends. That was it. He'd ducked all attempts made to interview him since his windfall. It was rumored that Adriana Gallant, an internet tabloid sensation with a reputation for perseverance, had her sights on him, but so far, with no luck.

Spending a night at the ranch had offered not one single new clue. He started work early in the mornings, so shortly after supper, he'd shown her to a bedroom at the far end of a very long hall, away from his own, and bade her good night. She had an en suite, an entertainment system, and a shelf full of reading material at her disposal. Then, right after breakfast, he'd driven her to the small local airport and flown her by helicopter to Billings himself, where she'd caught her flight home.

"I hired a private investigator," her father said.

Elizabeth, certain she hadn't heard her father correctly, ceased trying to zipper the overstuffed bag. "You did what?" She counted to three in her head. "Why would you do such a thing?"

"What did you expect me to do? My daughter is traveling across the country to live off the grid with a bunch of cowboys and juvenile delinquents. When I couldn't find anything on O'Connell through my business connections, I hired someone to do a more thorough search. The search came up empty. I forbid you to go."

Elizabeth took a deep breath. She'd been actively advocating for victims' rights since she was eighteen. She'd had her life threatened on two separate occasions. And yet, the case manager position in Montana was where her father decided to draw the line?

Of course, it was. Because he'd lose any sort of control. Both times she'd been threatened he'd hired bodyguards for her, and she hadn't protested because it was something he'd had to do for his mental health. She knew he loved her to the full extent of his capabilities, but he'd been so damaged by Marianne's murder that his capacity for expressing any strong feelings had atrophied. He kept them bottled up. Now she was moving too far away, to a place where he couldn't monitor her movements, and step in if he felt it was necessary, and he didn't like it.

But she had her own mental health to consider. She was twenty-nine years old and living at home. She'd stayed for their benefit, not hers, and that had to end.

He'd only react to negative emotion, however, and neither of them needed this fight. Besides, he was all bluster. Short of having her arrested or otherwise held captive, there wasn't much he could do to keep her from leaving.

"I won't be living off the grid," she said, maintaining calm. "A ranch is a twenty-four-hour operation. There are always people around. I'm trained to work with at-risk youth, and one of the Endeavour owners is the county sheriff, so I think I'll be fine."

"Do you honestly believe that a college degree and some small town 'barney' equal adequate protection?"

"I think guests will be arriving in a few minutes and I don't want to be late for my own party. Mom will send a search party for us if we don't hustle." Elizabeth finished wrestling with the bag's zipper and set the suitcase on the floor with the others. She bent to kiss her father's cheek. He wanted the best for her, and she loved him for it, but it changed nothing. "Are you coming, or are you going to sit here and risk her wrath?"

Thirty guests had been invited—most were friends of Elizabeth's, although a few belonged to her parents. One or two business acquaintances had been thrown in because

Theo liked to make clients feel like part of his inner circle. Meredith Benson wouldn't be pleased if she had to welcome them by herself.

Theo grumbled, but followed Elizabeth out of her bedroom suite, because he knew as well as she did who was really in charge of the family.

The Bensons lived in Lincoln Park, one of Chicago's better neighborhoods. Their home dated back to the early nineteenth century and had been in the family for generations. The original Bensons made their money off land speculation, and subsequent generations saw no reason not to carry on with tradition. Theo Benson owned a significant portion of the rental properties in Chicago's downtown business district.

Meredith waited for her husband and daughter in the great room that led to the outdoor patio on the main floor. High brick walls surrounded the patio for privacy, which in turn cut down on the cool, end-of-March winds, so they'd opened the doors and turned on the outside lights. A buffet had been set up on one side of the room with a bar at the end, where a bartender was setting out glasses and napkins.

Elizabeth supposed she'd look a lot like her mother in thirty years—but only if she decided to put in the hours at the gym and the spa. Meredith's red hair had been artificially deepened to auburn and she wore it in a discreet twist at her nape. Equally discreet makeup enhanced the barely discernable facial work she'd had done. She wore a black-and-white cocktail dress that showed off a dedication to physical fitness Elizabeth doubted she'd ever match. The height of her heels required a balance and grace most sixty-two-year-old women would envy.

Elizabeth's dress was a light, blushing pink with a low, draping neckline and a breezy skirt that came to mid-thigh and swirled around her legs when she moved. Her heels were as precarious as her mother's—a workaround for height-challenged women, her father liked to observe. She'd pinned her bright curls in a messy ponytail, and other than a pale lipstick that matched her dress, she wore no makeup at all.

"Did you talk to her?" Meredith asked Theo when he and Elizabeth approached.

"I did, but she refuses to listen to reason," he replied.

"I'm standing right here," Elizabeth said, without any great hopes. She was well used to having both parents ignore any input from her as they mapped out her life.

Yes, it was beyond time she moved out. The child-parent relationship they shared wasn't healthy. She never worried about herself. She weighed her options and did what was best for everyone involved—exactly as she was doing now, because parents shouldn't make life choices for adult children. They should be enjoying a stage in their marriage meant to be all about them.

Before Elizabeth could make any further attempts to insert herself into the conversation, the Milburns arrived. They were old family friends. Their eldest daughter had been a close friend of Marianne's. Elizabeth had grown up with their youngest son, Nathan. Nathan was blond, very metro, but enjoyed a coarse joke. Despite both families' attempts to encourage a closer relationship, they viewed each other as brother and sister and squabbled as such. Nathan had come out in his early twenties, putting an end to any matchmaking hopes. He lived with his partner, Phillip, in a condo near the Loop, Chicago's central business district.

Nathan cornered Elizabeth a few minutes after he'd been handed a drink.

"I've been asked to talk sense into you," he said. "Unfortunately, I don't see a downside to your move to Montana. You're finally getting away from your parents—you'll have to learn how to pay rent, by the way—and Montana is full of cowboys. So. Many. Cowboys. Phillip and I are already planning our visit."

"I'll be sure to tell everyone how hard you worked to convince me to change my mind," Elizabeth said, rolling her eyes.

She was a whole lot less interested in cowboys than she was in her research, particularly if Ryan O'Connell was a prime example. His looks and his money were about all he had going for him. He lacked even the most basic of social skills. He'd make an excellent case study for something or other, although she had yet to figure out what.

"Seriously, though. Are you really going through with this?" Nathan asked, with a hint of genuine concern. "Montana is so far away. I understand why your parents are worried, too. They've tolerated all the advocacy you've done, but you know as well as I do that taking a job working one-on-one with at-risk teenaged boys was guaranteed to trigger their buttons."

Yes, she was well aware. It hadn't escaped her notice that the boy they'd tried to push on her when she was old enough to date turned out to be gay, either.

"I took the job for me. Fighting for victims' rights was never going to be enough for me and you know it. I want to save lives, not pick up the pieces after the fact."

The room had begun to fill, and already, there were more than a few people trying to catch Elizabeth's eye. Since she was the guest of honor, continuing a private conversation was about to become impossible.

Nathan, too, noticed they'd become the center of attention.

"And I love you for it," he said, wrapping an arm around her shoulders and kissing her cheek. "Mom and Dad plan to keep an eye on your parents for you, so don't worry about them. But stay in touch, okay?"

Ryan

THE CONFERENCE ROOM for Grand's chamber of commerce

was overly warm and smelled of stale cigars, thanks to a loose interpretation of Montana's Clean Indoor Air Act and a ventilation system likely installed prior to 1889 and Montana becoming a state. The building itself, located next to the town library off Yellowstone Drive, had once served as a lodging house and dated back to Grand's founding in 1876, meaning as an historical site, any renovations were grudgingly and sparsely approved.

Ryan, at the lectern, checked the time on his phone with mounting, although carefully hidden, impatience. The new case manager had called from Bismarck, North Dakota, that morning to let him know she was taking the scenic route to Grand, but expected to arrive at the Endeavour by six o'clock.

He'd planned to be home before then, but the meeting had been running long even before he'd used up his allotted minutes explaining the Endeavour Ranch's application for a Professional Rodeo Cowboys Association-sanctioned rodeo. The chamber hosted an annual bucking horse sale that drew in large crowds and he'd hoped to leverage off it by getting the timing just right.

The executive committee apparently had nowhere better to be on a Friday night, because they asked plenty of questions, specifically regarding the effect a rodeo might have on local businesses already sponsoring events for the bucking horse sale. Fortunately, one benefit to being a billionaire was that the committee hadn't dismissed his proposal out of hand, even though he could see that several members wanted to do so—mainly because they owned the businesses supporting the horse sale. A few more simply didn't like change, particularly if there was nothing in it for them.

So, while he might not be getting the enthusiasm he'd have liked, he was also unlikely to receive much opposition, meaning he could move forward.

"The Endeavour Ranch is committed to furthering our philanthropic activities," Ryan concluded, wrapping up his presentation. "This rodeo will provide an opportunity for us to contribute back to the local community and to the state of Montana. We'll make all initial investments, and of course, local businesses will be given the opportunity to participate." He'd saved the best for last because he believed in ending any sales pitch on as high a note as possible. "And, to guarantee we get nation-wide publicity, the Endeavour has hired Miles Decker to be our spokesman."

That got their attention. Decker had been one of the top professional bull riders in the PBR, and the face of professional bull riding for the past three years, until his famous face was badly scarred in a publicity stunt. He'd made it widely known that he planned to retire from public life.

What Ryan didn't mention was how he'd also promised Decker the space and the financial backing to begin his own bull breeding program, because it did compete with a local business that already had one up and running, and would definitely create some hard feelings.

The meeting wrapped up and Ryan began a sedate but determined dash for the door, doing his best to dodge those tenacious executive members wanting to chat, without appearing to be in too much of a hurry. The day had been a balmy sixty degrees and he'd had men out fencing the area surrounding the badlands, which was about as much fun as it sounded. They'd be tired and hungry when they landed, and judging by some of the nastygrams regarding his parentage he'd received via handheld two-way radio, out of sorts as well.

He'd go home, smooth some delicate feathers, get the new case manager installed in her bunkhouse, then race back to Grand in time to attend the hospital fundraiser at the Grand Master Brewery and Taproom. Dallie's fundraiser was the evening's priority.

He made it to the parking lot and his car and he slid into the driver's seat with a sense of contentment. He liked cars—the faster, the better—and he'd owned the steel-blue Mercedes AMG since before he'd had billions of dollars dumped in his lap. He loved the car because he'd earned it himself.

Of course, he'd loved every car he'd ever stolen as a kid for the same reason, too—he'd gotten such an adrenaline rush from scouting them out, monitoring the owners' routines, doing his research, choosing his moment... As a kid, he'd truly believed he'd earned every one of those joyrides.

The cars he'd bought with the blood money were toys.

He let Dallas and Dan drive whichever one of those struck their fancy. He had no personal attachment to them. This car, however...

The AMG was his baby. Nobody drove it but him.

A quick check of the clock on the dashboard made him wince. He was late. What were the chances that Elizabeth Benson might be late, too?

Slim to none, as it turned out.

He arrived at the ranch at six forty-eight to find a late-model, metallic-gray BMW coupe with an Illinois license plate parked next to the garage. He couldn't resist checking it out.

As he walked around it, he let out a low whistle of appreciation. Elizabeth Benson didn't live on a social worker's salary if this was her ride. It was no base model either, although she'd opted for a color that didn't draw a whole lot of attention. The car was expensive without being ostentatious—a lot like Elizabeth herself.

Who was nowhere to be seen.

He hunched his shoulders against the chill evening wind, bringing the wool lining of his trench coat into alignment with the back of his neck. Her car was crammed full of suitcases and bags, but she wasn't waiting anywhere near it. A quick check informed him she wasn't in the house, either.

She clearly didn't know how to stay put, and he didn't like the idea of a city girl roaming the ranch unescorted. What with moving equipment, and the bull pen nearby—

whose fence was more of a suggestion than useful for actual containment—accidents were known to occur, even when a person was familiar with safety procedures.

He should have told her to wait here for him when he'd spoken to her that morning. Better yet, he should have called someone to be here to greet her when he saw he was running late.

But part of him was a bit of a stubborn ass, or so he'd been told, and having her forced on him brought the ass part to the forefront. He'd been harboring hopes she'd change her mind once she got here and be gone by the end of her first week—or maybe her second, since she'd held her own during her interview, even when it must have been obvious that he didn't want her—and he planned to do nothing to make her job easy.

As for her drive from Illinois to Montana at the end of March, either she hadn't learned a thing from her blizzard experience of a few weeks ago, or she was completely without fear. Perhaps a little of both.

Either way, he was annoyed that he had to go looking for her, even though he was the one behind schedule. He had a half hour to find her and get her settled. He fired off a quick text to Dallas to give him an update on his ETA at the fundraiser. Then, he set off on his quest. The lights were on in the cookhouse, which was attached to the machine shed, so he decided to start there.

He'd already been half annoyed when he walked in. The

sight that greeted him escalated it to ninety-five percent.

The counter that divided the eating area from the kitchen was piled high with dirty dishes and the smell of seared meat lingered, suggesting they'd grilled burgers for dinner. None of that was extraordinary.

The tables that had been pushed back and the chairs shoved aside, clearing a space in the center of the room, was where things diverged. Furthermore, Young John, who towered head and shoulders above dainty, ladylike little Elizabeth, had an arm wrapped around her throat while Steve and Handy, the two idiots who were also about to get fired, cheered him on.

Ryan saw red.

"What the hell is going on here?" he demanded.

Chapter Four

Elizabeth

ELIZABETH HAD ARRIVED at the Endeavour Ranch promptly on schedule only to find that, despite having called ahead to ensure she was expected, once again, she'd been forgotten.

A lesser woman might take it personally, but she'd decided that her reclusive new boss had issues with women in general that had very little to do with her. How deep those issues ran she couldn't be sure, so rather than wait around for him, as he likely intended, she again went off in search of signs of life.

She'd found the ranch hands eating their dinners, and once she'd explained who she was and why she was here, they'd invited her to join them. Since they were now her coworkers, she thought she might as well get to know them. One thing had led to another, and…

Well.

Naturally, Heathcliff would choose the worst possible moment to make an appearance.

Young John—whose name, in actual fact, was John Young—dropped the chokehold and backed away from her, but slowly, as if afraid he might trigger a wild animal attack. Elizabeth could hardly fault him for his use of discretion. Ryan had a feral, bone-chilling look in his dark eyes and a tenseness to his body that did, indeed, indicate predatory aggression.

She leaped in to defuse the situation.

"Hello," she said brightly. She straightened the hem of her shirt and dusted off the seat of her jeans. "We were having a teambuilding moment and I was showing the men how to do a rolling knee bar." Sort of.

John had assured her all of the hands on the ranch were at her disposal if she had difficulties with her young charges and she'd informed him she could take care of herself. They expressed polite disbelief—she was impressed by their nice manners as they went about it—and she'd been more than happy to prove it to them. It was all in good fun until Heathcliff showed up.

"A teambuilding moment," Ryan echoed. She didn't need her degree to pick up on his opinion. What a shame that a man as at ease in a trench coat and business suit as he was in stained coveralls should be so dark and dour, personality-wise.

"She already threw me once, but only because she caught me off guard. I bet her she couldn't take Young John down, now that he's seen how she does it," Handy overexplained, possibly risking death, since the velociraptor's focus shifted to him. He stuck his hands in his pockets and jiggled from one foot to the other. He was one of the two young men she'd met in the machine shop when she was looking for Ryan the day of her interview. Steve, who'd wisely kept quiet, was the other.

"Would you like a demonstration?" Elizabeth said to Ryan, as if offering to toss her boss on his duff was an everyday occurrence for her. "You never know when you might need to defend yourself in a dark alley."

"Because everyone hangs out in dark alleys," Ryan said dryly. Then, he surprised her. He shrugged. "Why not?"

She hadn't expected him to agree. Now things were weird.

He stripped off his trench coat and tossed it over a chair. He stepped up behind her and crooked his elbow around her throat. He pressed her against a whole lot of work-hardened body, reinforcing how much bigger he was than her.

His grip scrambled her brain. The warm scent of the crisp cotton sleeve so close to her nose created a second distraction. It smelled of lemon laundry detergent, a hint of the disinfectant used in the calving shed—which wasn't at all unpleasant—and a maleness unique to him, reminding her of the night of the storm and the sweater he'd loaned her. It was amazing how much power the human sense of smell held when it came to association. A sense of trust in him filled her, which made no sense of all, because there was absolutely nothing about the tension in him right at this moment that should make her feel safe.

The discovery that he'd made such a positive impression on her—or on her subconscious, at least—was unsettling. Maybe it wasn't unusual, though, given she also associated him with bringing a new life into the world. Women, whether through societal pressures or natural instinct, tended to rank nurturing high as a positive trait.

Plus, he was hot. That was hard to forget.

"Whenever you're ready, Houdini," Ryan muttered into her ear, disrupting her self-analysis.

You asked for it, Heathcliff.

She sagged, using her body weight to drag herself lower, and thrust her jaw into the crook of his arm. She jerked down with her hands at the same time, then rammed an elbow into his midsection while she stomped on his instep with her heel. She slid her shoulder into his armpit and pulled one of his arms forward, rolling him over her hip to land on his back on the floor.

She landed with him, and immediately flipped around, wedging her thigh between his, and jammed it hard against his groin. She grabbed his left leg, arched her hip into his kneecap, and jerked backward, hard, but not hard enough to do any damage to the joint.

But that was where things went awry. Elizabeth, already smaller and lighter than he was, hadn't taken dirty play into consideration. He slid a hand over her buttocks from his position behind and beneath her, inserted it between her legs where she straddled his thigh, then cupped an intimate part of her body in a bold move no one had ever tried on her in any class she'd ever taken. She relaxed her grip on his leg, shocked, and before she could recover, she was on her back on the floor and he had her arms and legs pinned while he sat on her stomach. He immediately released her, jumping up to pull her to her feet.

Her hot face had to be beet red, and not from exertion. *Ever hear of the #MeToo movement, buddy?*

"Find yourselves a new teambuilding exercise," Ryan advised everyone present. His glower made him seem all the more feral and her three coworkers flinched. "First and last warning. The next man who puts his hands on a female employee for anything other than a life-saving emergency is fired. Elizabeth." He rounded on her. A sinking sensation dislodged her stomach from its proper location. "Let's take a walk. I'd like to speak to you in private."

And wasn't she off to a great start in her new, probably short-lived, position?

"Thanks for dinner. Let me know when it's my turn to cook," she said to the men. Her face was still flaming—the curse of redheads the world over—even though she wasn't the one who'd done something wrong.

She picked up her coat from one of the chairs and followed Ryan to the cookhouse door. He held it open for her, which threw her off, because the action was so gentlemanly, and he'd just behaved anything but.

She stepped outside. A stiff wind carried the soft lowing of mothers calling to babies from the pastures nearest the ranch. The sound filled her heart, while air, several degrees cooler even though the sun hadn't yet set, soothed her hot cheeks. He'd rattled her. That didn't happen very often.

"You cheated," she accused him, even though it made her sound childish, because she preferred to attack rather than wait to defend. They had that in common, although their power dynamic was definitely unbalanced. She scurried to keep up with his longer stride. If she thought there was anything even remotely sexual about what he'd done, they'd be having a far different conversation.

He cast her a sidelong look of amusement, which she resented. "Damn straight I did. How many men—or teenaged boys, for that matter—do you think will play fair in a real-life situation?"

"Don't worry. Next time, I'll break your leg," she said, with feeling.

A smile played with his lips, making him look moderately less terrifying. "If you ever try that move on a man for real, see that you do. But for what it's worth, I don't believe you could do it."

What she couldn't believe was that she was about to defend her ability to break someone's leg. The man was a barbarian, and so, she responded in kind. "Don't discount me because I'm a woman. I'm stronger than I look."

"It's got nothing to do with your size, your gender, or your physical strength," he said. "Most people don't have the capacity to harm another human being. The civilized part of the brain throws a switch and warns you to stop what you're doing and reassess your emotional response. You're normal."

She knew all of that. But he acted as if human decency were some sort of defect, and she wouldn't be in her profession if she didn't trust in its power.

"I disagree. I believe the majority of people react to direct violent stimuli in one of three ways. Fight or flight are the first two. The third reaction is to try and reason. To bargain your way out of the situation."

He stopped so abruptly she bumped into him. "And how does bargaining usually work out for women?" he asked quietly, the smile gone. He didn't say it, for which she was grateful, but she could read it in his expression—*How did it work out for your sister?*

Her chest burned. A visceral pain she'd thought long-buried threatened to burst free. She fought it back. Thinking about Marianne's final moments did no one any good. A million responses ran through her head, not one of them appropriate to say to her boss.

The boss who'd groped her in front of three men.

"No more impromptu 'teambuilding' exercises," he said. "If you find yourself in a position where you have to use a rolling knee bar on someone, don't waste energy trying to reason with them, either. You break that leg, Elizabeth.

Don't think twice about it. That's an order." He didn't wait for her to answer but began walking again. "Now come on. I'll show you where you'll be staying so you can unpack and get settled in."

Ryan

RYAN HAD HELPED Elizabeth unload her car because he wasn't asking one of those douchebags to do it.

As a consequence, he was running late.

The road from the Endeavour Ranch meandered the same path as the Tongue River, which emptied into the Yellowstone River not far from the Lucky Lil Casino. The casino and the taproom serviced far different clientele, although both businesses were hotbeds of activity most nights.

Hannah Brand had set up the Grand Master Brewery and Taproom on the outskirts of town in a small residential neighborhood populated by an eclectic mix of people, giving it a strong hipster vibe. Many were first-time home buyers just starting their families. Others were retirees who didn't require a whole lot of space. She'd wanted to give her business the feel of an old English pub where the neighborhood gathered, but also to offer people something to occupy them while they were there, so she'd added board games.

The drive from the Endeavour to the taproom normally took twenty minutes. Ryan made it in fifteen. The small parking lot behind the taproom was full when he arrived, forcing him to park a few blocks away. He jogged the short distance.

The incident with Elizabeth was fresh in his mind. There was a good chance he'd overreacted. The men already thought him hard and unreasonable. But at the sight of her, restrained and defenseless, he'd become seven years old again, peering in terror through stair rails, while his mother, screaming below, was forced to watch his dad being murdered.

Bargaining had gotten her nothing.

Such was the life of a Chicago mobster's daughter married to the mob's light-fingered accountant. He'd been an amazing dad, and Ryan held tight to what few memories of him he had, but his life choices had been questionable at best. One would think the crooked accountant cliché alone should have been deterrent enough. His mother believed he'd been set up, but Ryan was never so sure. Little bits and pieces of conversations he'd been privy to—because no one paid attention to children—had surfaced during countless sessions with child psychologists.

God, how he hated Giaco the "Jackal" Cienetti. It was especially galling that his grandfather died in his sleep, the cold, arrogant old bastard. Hopefully, he'd face judgment in the afterlife, because there'd been no justice served against him on earth.

He skidded to a halt at the Grand Master Brewery's front door and squeezed white-knuckled fingers around the brass door handle. He'd go in, gladhand for the appropriate amount of time, and get out. The whole Elizabeth issue had left him in a bad mood, so it wasn't as if he'd be a whole lot of fun.

"Mr. O'Connell," a woman called out. He looked around and a bright light flashed in his face.

He blinked to clear his vision. He recognized her— Adriana Gallant, a television tabloid reporter trapped in a forty-something-year-old woman's body. Some men might find her even features, sleek hair and clothes, and toned legs attractive. He thought she was plastic and lacking in character. She held her phone in her hand with the video on, angled to capture the encounter.

"This is a private event," he said tersely, and jerked the door open. He closed it in her face and fought off the urge to lock it behind him.

She's only interested in the story behind three brand-new billionaires and the Endeavour Ranch. She'd never be able to follow the trail back to Chicago. He was confident of that. He'd looked for it himself over the years so he could be sure.

He shook off the encounter and hung his coat on the coatrack next to the entry.

The fundraiser turnout was good, considering the venue was small. The taproom seated thirty comfortably, could accommodate sixty standing, and appeared to be close to capacity. He recognized quite a few of the people, even though he didn't hang out much in town.

Zack McGregor, a close friend of Dan's, was here with his wife. Posey McGregor was rumored to be an heir to a fortune worth more than the Endeavour's, although no one would guess it by looking at her. She was blond, and pretty enough, but in an understated, backup singer kind of way. Not like fiery, beautiful, red-haired Elizabeth at all, who—thanks to her teambuilding session—he couldn't get out of his head.

Weldon Scott, who owned the Running River Ranch, had also made an appearance. He wasn't much liked in Grand and rumors circulated about his tense relationship with the three McGregor brothers, who owned the Wagging Tongue Ranch next to his. Weldon and Zack were on speaking terms, but Jake, the oldest McGregor, and Luke, next in line, both kept their distance. Ryan didn't see Jake or Luke anywhere, and hadn't expected to. He scanned the room for Dallas and Dan.

Dan, who never seemed in a hurry, stood near the bar with an arm around Jazz, the leggy blond base manager who ran the Endeavour's seasonal smoke jumping operation. They'd been a couple for almost two years now, and whenever their lives settled down, were headed for marriage.

Dallas was working the room, which Ryan knew wasn't his favorite thing, but this was his event, and he was the guest of honor. He glided easily from one group to the next, but his eyes flitted continually to Hannah, the adorable brunette behind the bar, and Ryan found no fault in that. Hannah was as sweet as she was pretty, and their relationship was as solid as Dan and Jazz's, although mainly because Dallie, like an eager, overgrown puppy, never knew when to give up. Obliviousness had worked well for him in this instance.

Ryan was happy that his friends had found partners who cared more about them than their money. Dan and Dallas weren't all that comfortable with their newfound wealth and didn't have the faintest idea of how to protect themselves. Dallas, in particular, liked to give it away—which was the whole plan, yes—although not necessarily to give it away, so much as to put it to good use.

He'd missed Dallie's speech, which was unfortunate, but not the end of the world. The clinic would get its money. He'd already written a sizeable check on the Endeavour's behalf.

He worked his way toward the bar, pausing to speak to a few people—Zack McGregor in particular. He liked the youngest McGregor. On the surface, he seemed as laidback as Dan. After a few business dealings with him, however, Ryan discovered Zack had a practical, ruthless streak a whole lot like his own, except Zack's came from a better gene pool. He knew where lines should be drawn whereas Ryan knew better than to leave his to chance.

One more reason to hate the old Jackal. He had a terrifying fear of turning out like him, which was the biggest reason
why he'd drawn his unsuspecting friends into the inheritance
with him. He relied on Dan and Dallas to keep his ethics in
check.

"Hey, Ryan," Zack said.

Posey smiled politely and slid a little closer to her husband. Ryan knew he frightened her, but there wasn't much
he could do about it. If anything, he found her timidity
around him exasperating.

Elizabeth, who should be, wasn't afraid of him in the
least.

Zack hugged his wife to his side and kept right on talking. "Any truth to the rumor the Endeavour Ranch plans to
host a PRCA-sanctioned rodeo and you've hired Miles
Decker as spokesman?"

He'd expected word to get out fast in a small town like
Grand, but two hours had to be some sort of record. "It's all
true. Planning to enter?"

Zack laughed. "Those days are behind me, I'm afraid. I
tried bull riding once and once was enough. I've got a family
to think of these days." He smiled proudly at Posey, who
beamed back. "Number three's on the way."

The McGregor brothers were big into family, something
Ryan had very little personal experience with, and even less
interest in, given his roots, but he admired loyalty. Jake had
custody of their sister's three children after she and her

husband, and the senior McGregors, were all killed in a plane crash. Zack and Luke had come home to help out and ended up staying.

"Congratulations," Ryan said.

There wasn't much else he could think of to say. The hell with the gladhanding. There were too many happy couples in here and he needed a drink. Elizabeth had rattled him and he wasn't good at small talk to begin with.

He said goodbye to Zack and Posey and went to the bar.

"What took you so long?" Dan asked when he sidled up.

"I was talking to Zack and his wife. Hi, Jazz," Ryan added, peering around Dan to greet his friend's better half.

Jazz's polite smile held even less warmth for him than Posey's. No question about it. He had a real way with women.

"Not what I meant. You were only planning to show the new case manager to her bunkhouse," Dan said. He leaned back, hanging both elbows on the bar behind him. Lazy blue eyes—which weren't nearly as lazy as unsuspecting people might think—homed in on him. "Problems?"

It was a matter of perspective. Dan likely wouldn't see it in the same light Ryan did, so he dodged the question. "I got held up at the chamber of commerce meeting by a few dissenters, but dropping Miles Decker's name did the trick." He scanned Hannah's menu. She had a maple-based beer on tap that he liked, but it packed quite a punch. "If I have a few drinks, can I catch a ride home with you?"

"It's up to Jazz. She has the keys."

Jazz lifted a toned shoulder to indicate her indifference, which was about as much enthusiasm as she worked up when she was forced to interact with Ryan. It was his own fault that she didn't like him, he acknowledged. He'd had her investigated when Dan began to get serious and she hadn't been happy when she found out—mainly because her gene pool didn't contain much more to be proud of than his— although it turned out Jazz herself was plenty good enough for his friend.

"We're all going to the same place," she said.

Dan, who thought it was funny that she didn't like Ryan, tried to rein in his grin. *It's all on you, buddy*, that wiseass grin informed him.

It was. He'd do it all over again, too. He didn't let very many people get close to him and he took good care of the ones who did. Dallas and Dan were at the top of the list.

He caught Hannah's eye and flagged her over. "I'll take a large glass of the maple," he said. "Maybe bring me a pitch-er."

After Elizabeth and Adriana Gallant, he'd need it.

Chapter Five

Elizabeth

ELIZABETH HAD SPENT the better part of her first month clearing up the last of the red tape so the group home could open its doors.

It was now May.

Two counselors had been hired, Colin and Ace, both young men with ranch experience who'd double as cowhands and share bunkhouses with their young charges. Elizabeth had one of the smaller bunkhouses—the one closest to the ranch house—to herself. Handy told her it was used mainly for the younger family members of Dallas and Dan whenever they came to stay.

Discreet inquiries determined Ryan had no family other than a mother who'd passed away almost a decade ago, which might explain why he was such a loner. Elizabeth wondered if they'd been close and how her death had affected him.

She'd been assigned an office next to his in the ranch house. She closed the last of the case files she'd been reviewing and drummed her fingers on her desk as she stared thoughtfully through the glass-paneled wall overlooking the central lounge. Four of the ten boys accepted into the program had arrived on Monday. Two more would arrive in two weeks' time, then two more every second week throughout June.

She was a little appalled by how much labor Ryan expected of them. It seemed he took the tough-love approach to child rearing. She pushed away from her desk.

They should talk.

He was in his office. The glare of his computer screen reflected off a pair of glasses that lent him a more scholarly air and added another facet to his complex personality. The jeans and casual shirt he wore were expensive and deepened the mystery. She had yet to figure him out—other than that he could be prickly when things didn't go the way he expected or planned. The best approach in dealing with him was head-on and to stand strong.

She tapped one knuckle on his open door. "May I come in?"

His chin rose a fraction. He aimed it in her general direction. Bemused eyes flickered away from the computer screen for the briefest of seconds. Untidy brown hair sported trails where fingers had raked through it. "Sure."

Then again, now might not be the best time. Whatever he was working on appeared to require his undivided attention. "I can come back later." She prepared to retreat.

"Wait." He removed the glasses, tossed them on his desk, and rubbed his eyes. He indicated the chair across from him. "Sit. What's up?"

She smoothed the skirt of her dress and sat, knees together, her stiletto-clad feet crossed at the ankles and tucked under her chair. She'd embraced the ranch's standard jeans-and-coveralls uniform for her morning start feeding babies, but hadn't yet been able to come to terms with the almost equally casual dress code during office hours.

"The workload you've laid out for the boys," she began. "It seems somewhat..." She searched for the right word. *Harsh. Unrealistic. Excessive.* "Heavy, considering they'll also have schoolwork to complete. Montana's child labor law states children sixteen to seventeen must work outside of school hours, and between seven in the morning and seven at night, for a total of eighteen hours per week during the school year."

His brows slammed together. "I assume you've read their files. These aren't exactly top-tier students we're talking about."

His reaction to her concern was hardly encouraging. Nevertheless, she persevered. She couldn't complete her six-month probation and feel she'd done her best for these boys by tiptoeing around his opinions when hers were backed up by research and law. Besides, he'd seen something of value in them or they wouldn't be here. They deserved a genuine chance.

"And they're never going to become good students if they don't have the time or energy for their studies," she said.

"Our goal is to provide therapy, supervision, and structure in order to keep them on the right side of the law. We can worry about their academic performance later. They're all smart. They'll catch up."

"Part of their therapy involves them learning to properly interact with their peers. Six of the boys can function in the local public school system, which is where I recommend they be placed. They can't go to school all day, get their studies in, then spend eight hours doing hard labor, too."

Ryan folded his arms and tipped back in his chair. "Think of it as chores, not labor. Maybe on-the-job training. Better yet, let's call it extracurricular activities. Believe it or not, a lot of teenaged boys consider working on a ranch fun. For that matter, some women do, too. I haven't heard you complain about feeding the orphans at six o'clock every morning." A glimmer of amusement sparked shards the color of iced coffee crystals in his eyes.

"That's different," she said, proving how much he rattled her when he smiled, because what kind of educated rebuttal was that?

"Really? How so?"

Because she was an adult. Because she found the ranch to be an exciting adventure. "Because I'm not a seventeen-year-old boy."

"No, you're not. I used to be one, though. Maybe you should see them in action before you pass judgment. It might change your opinion." He threw it down like a challenge.

Challenge accepted.

"It might at that." She doubted it, but he appeared to derive a great deal of pleasure from arguing and she had no intention of being obstinate simply so he could have fun. Especially when it came at her expense. "Why don't I join the two mucking out the horse stalls tomorrow morning?" she suggested.

Ryan owned eleven Tennessee Walkers, a breed known for its four-beat running walk. She had no idea what any of that meant, but she did know the horses were lovely. She'd been introduced to them on the weekend, shortly after a newborn palomino foal rounded off the herd count to twelve, and was secretly disappointed that its mother showed no signs of abandoning it. That didn't mean she wanted to shovel out their stable.

Let's see how much joy that activity brings to teenaged boys' lives.

"Great idea," he said, because it was too much to hope for that he could ever admit he was wrong. "We'll see you around seven then, right after you finish feeding the orphans. They should still be at it. Normally, one of the hands could have the stalls mucked out in an hour, but as I said, we're not running a prison camp. The kids have likely never used a pitchfork, before. There's a learning curve for us all and I expect it will take them a lot longer than average for the first week or so."

"How very reasonable of you."

"Thanks."

What a smug—

He frustrated her to no end.

But he wasn't wrong simply because he disagreed with her assessment. As long as the boys weren't being physically or mentally abused, she had no real grounds for complaint. They were here because they hadn't thrived in a traditional environment. Perhaps a different mix of schooling and work really would have a more positive effect.

She spent the remainder of the day in her office, not quite out of sorts, but not satisfied with the outcome of their talk, either. She ate her dinner in the cookhouse with Young John, who seemed impervious to Ryan's threats, and the two counselors, Colin and Ace. Two teens had been assigned kitchen duty along with Handy and Steve. Their facial expressions conveyed their lack of enthusiasm. Since they knew they weren't here for a vacation, and KP was rotational, she was unsympathetic.

After eating her burger and salad—prepared under conditions best not scrutinized too closely—she took a long bath in her bunkhouse, watched television for an hour, then went to bed with a good book she'd been longing to finish.

She tried to sleep with her window open, but wasn't yet

used to the noises the ranch made at night and they still felt unnatural. She'd never had an overactive imagination before coming to Montana. Now, every rustle of the shrubs under her window had her wondering about bears and the thickness of the walls.

When she did fall asleep, however, it was her boss, not the night noises, that bothered her dreams.

THE NEXT MORNING, she fed the last of the newborns a few minutes before seven, then crossed the yard between the calving pen and the stables. The horses lingered in the paddock outside. The new foal kicked up its heels, sticking close to its patient mother.

The stable doors had been thrown back at either end, allowing fresh air to circulate the entire length of the concrete center walkway, carrying odors of dust, horse, and wet straw in its wake. Something soft crumbled under her boot. Ew. She didn't check to see what it was in case it might once have been alive.

She'd half-expected Ryan to be waiting for her, but he was nowhere in sight, which was likely for the best. No matter how good her intentions, she seemed to rub him the wrong way. He rubbed her the wrong way too, although she didn't think he had any good intentions at all.

The two boys assigned to the job had no adult supervision, she noted with disapproval. For a man who believed in making them work for their room and board, Ryan had a lax approach to enforcing the rules.

The boys began to complain the moment she walked in.

"I thought there were child labor laws in this country," Tyce said, proving Ryan was right and these boys weren't slow.

Tyce, a petty thief who'd progressed from shoplifting to breaking and entering, had opted out of the foster care system at sixteen without any other means of support. He was tall and blond, with a severe case of acne that would likely clear up in a few years. When it did, he'd be a heartbreaker. He scraped a forkful of detritus and limp hay into a wheelbarrow manned by another one of the teens.

Angel, his partner, was living proof that not all parents hit the mark when naming their children. He looked the part well enough, so that was likely what had misled them. Stockier than Tyce, with startling, pale-green eyes offset by a light-brown complexion and curly, walnut-brown hair, he'd been caught in an affair with one of his teachers, for which she'd rightly been fired. He'd retaliated by trashing the principal's office. His caseworker had tacked a note to his file saying he had borderline narcissistic tendencies. Elizabeth suspected that was professional polite-speak for a self-entitled, spoiled little brat with an ego to match. His family was upper middle class and had likely bailed him out of trouble numerous times before giving up.

Yet she knew very well that coming from money didn't preclude problems at home. If anything, money made the problems easier to hide.

"Speak for yourself," Angel told Tyce. "I'm a man, not a child." He ran a bold gaze over Elizabeth's coverall-clad body, as if making his point.

Since Elizabeth was zippered inside enough tough navy cotton to satisfy the sensibilities of a nineteenth-century nun, and her green rubber boots didn't scream sexy either, she ignored his attempt to provoke a reaction when it only served to reinforce that he really was more boy than man.

"You're welcome to take up your concerns with Sheriff McKillop, although I'm not sure he'll agree with your interpretation of what constitutes child labor," Elizabeth said frankly. Dan, as the sheriff, and Dallas, as the group home's health care services provider, and also as co-owners of the Endeavour, had each been briefed on the residents and their respective backgrounds. "You do realize that twelve-year-old girls muck out stalls at riding schools, don't you?"

"Why don't you grab a fork and help out, then?" Angel said.

"Because this is your assignment, not mine. I've finished my chores."

They grumbled a bit more before returning to work.

A ramp, fashioned out of two long planks of wood, rested against the bed of a truck at the far end of the stable. Angel ran the loaded wheelbarrow to the top of the ramp and wrestled it onto its side, dumping the contents into the bed.

Elizabeth closed her eyes and whispered a one-word, single-syllabled prayer. So many safety violations…

Someone touched her shoulder. Her eyes jolted open and her heart kicked into a live demonstration of the running gait that Tennessee Walkers were apparently so famous for. She rounded on her assailant—and her heart began to race for a whole different reason.

This, boys, is a man.

"Did no one ever tell you it's wrong to sneak up on a woman?" she demanded, hand on her chest, completely rattled by now.

Ryan took a step back and threw his palms in the air. He stared at her as if she'd lost her mind. "Why—because you might try your rolling knee bar maneuver on me again?"

She had no comeback for that.

Tyce, who'd witnessed their face-off, began to laugh, even though he wasn't in on the entire joke. Ryan shifted his attention to him. "If you and Angel would both use pitchforks and take turns dumping the wheelbarrow, you'd be done twice as fast."

Tyce spread the love by glaring at Angel, who trotted up with the now-empty wheelbarrow. "That's what I told him we should do."

Angel skidded to a halt, unconcerned. "My way is faster because I'm stronger."

"You aren't stronger than me, little man." Tyce propped his pitchfork against the side of the stall, tines down, and squared off as if preparing to settle their difference of opinion the old-fashioned way.

Ryan pushed between them, retrieved the abandoned pitchfork, and thrust it into Tyce's hands. "You. Get back to work." He turned on Angel. "You. Go get another fork. If the two of you aren't done here in half an hour, no one is saving breakfast for you."

Angel, to his credit, did as he was told, although if his swagger was meant to annoy Tyce, it accomplished its purpose. Tyce, it appeared, had a short fuse. Good to know.

"Arming them doesn't seem wise," Elizabeth whispered to Ryan. "And that makeshift ramp they're using isn't safe either," she felt compelled to point out.

Ryan's scowl deepened. Irritation spun in a dark cloud around him as he glowered at her. "Why are you even here?"

Welcome back, Heathcliff. She raised her eyebrows, drew her chin back, and skewered him with one of the infamous stares she'd learned from her mother. He had no business getting snippy with her. She was an innocent bystander, doing her job. "Because you wanted me to see how happy the boys are with their extracurricular activities, remember?"

"Jesus." He scrubbed his hands up and down his face. "Let's go eat. I'll send Colin to referee."

Ryan

ELIZABETH STARTED IN on him the second they emerged from the stable.

"A ranch is hardly a safe work environment, particularly for someone who's never worked on one before and doesn't know what to expect. Why wasn't anyone supervising those boys?"

Ryan inhaled. The sweet, earthy smell of approaching rain filled his lungs. He loved a good storm and it looked as if they were in for one any minute. Fat-bellied clouds inched across a morning sky slowly turning to gray. A haze in the distance said it had already begun and was sweeping their way. The temperature dipped with its approach.

He focused on anything to distract him from how crazy Elizabeth made him. He'd never survive the remaining four and a half months of her probation. Not that he was counting the days. He shortened his stride enough for her to keep up—as long as she worked for it.

"Because they aren't little kids and I'm not starting off by treating them as if they are, or as if they can't be trusted," he said, in response to her question.

"Um..." Elizabeth's pretty amber eyes voiced her opinion on that.

"You don't think they should be trusted?" He would have thought she'd be all for giving them the benefit of the doubt. He was the only person she seemed to have zero faith in—which proved her instincts weren't one hundred percent off.

"Of course, I think they should be trusted. I'm surprised that you do," she said.

"Oh, I don't," he assured her, glancing down at her lovely face and the topknot of red curls. She looked adorable in her coveralls, which hadn't been the goal when he'd ordered them, but no one could claim they were suggestive. A tendril of hair had sprung free of the knot and clung to the curve of her throat like a question mark. "Everything of value is either locked up or kept under wraps"—case in point being the attractive woman beside him—"including the keys to the ATVs in the shed. The garage for the cars is always kept locked. The buildings are all equipped with security cameras. We're miles from anywhere. If anyone tries to run away, they'll have to steal a horse. Since none of them can ride yet, we'll worry about that particular pony once it's been saddled."

She crinkled her nose. "Funny."

"I thought so." He combed his brain for the right segue into the next topic, which was somewhat more sensitive, but since he wasn't good at sensitive, he gave up and jumped in. "You might want to be extra careful around Angel."

"Thank you for your concern, but I know all about the teacher he was involved with, if that's what you mean. I have his file, too."

So much important information never made it into those

files. He was being overprotective, even though she was a professional and had a background that made her warier than most, but he couldn't help it. He didn't have it in him to stand by while potential disasters unfolded.

"Do you also know about his friend's mother, the wife of a business acquaintance of his father, and a local librarian?" he asked.

"No... Those details weren't included in the files given to me. I'm curious as to where you got them?" The crook of an eyebrow indicated she expected an answer, but when he didn't offer her one, she carried on. "Although the only thing that truly surprises me is that he knows a librarian. I feel confident I can resist his charms."

He was a whole lot less confident that Angel, who liked older women, could resist hers. "I'm more concerned that your self-defense classes are only so good."

"You mean because I didn't take you down when you snuck up behind me just now?" she asked. "It wasn't exactly a dark alley situation."

Her smile knocked his thoughts out of whack. "I didn't sneak up on you." Not on purpose, although it depended on one's perspective, he supposed. He pulled his brain back into its rightful position. "For what it's worth, you'd be better off avoiding dark alley situations altogether. You don't exactly have the instincts of a Georges St-Pierre."

The next thing he knew he was on his back on the ground, looking up at the sky, as the first drops of rain spit in his face. A sharp rock ground its way under his left shoulder blade.

Elizabeth leaned over him, her hands on her thighs. "Sure I do. All I require is the right motivation."

"Happy to be of service." He'd set himself up for that so it was hard to be mad. Not at her, anyway.

He got up, dusted dirt and gravel off the seat of his jeans, then took a quick look around. Angel and Tyce were still in the stable. The other boys had gone to the cookhouse for breakfast. Most of the hands were out in the pastures. The yard was a ghost town. No one had witnessed the tiny powder keg flipping him onto his ass. He'd love to get her into a gym where there'd be no risk of real harm. She wouldn't stand a chance. He rubbed the sore spot on his shoulder. Not much of one, anyway.

Slim fingertips scored the flesh on his wrist. Anxious amber eyes sought out his. "Did I hurt you?"

"I think I've lost the use of my arm." He let it hang limp at his side for added effect.

She rolled her eyes. "Don't be such a baby."

So much for compassion. "Please. Don't hold back. Tell me what you really think of me."

A dimple in one cheek flashed in and out of existence. "It might be best if I don't."

"That hasn't stopped you so far." She'd had no trouble vocalizing any of her opinions to date. If she cared that he was her boss, no one would be able to tell. She certainly didn't offer him much respect.

Yet, while she frustrated him—he liked getting things done and her constant questions and insistence on rules slowed everything down—she was the only person other than Dan and Dallas who challenged him directly anymore.

He didn't like to be challenged. Neither, however, did he like to be bored. She wasn't boring—he'd give her that. To make things more interesting, she was exceptionally pretty in the coveralls and those Barbie doll-sized rubber boots. He wished he'd ordered them in pink so he could find out her opinion.

An urge to kiss her struck hard. An itch to run a thumb across her cheek to find out if her skin was as soft as it looked followed hot on its heels. He leaned forward a fraction. There was no one around. No one would know if he kissed her. He had a hunch she might not object, even though the power dynamics between them were skewed in his favor.

But it baffled him somewhat to find he was attracted to her. He usually preferred a sure thing—someone easy to bed and easy to shed—who had no expectations of any long-term or permanent commitments, because he had no intentions of extending his gene pool. Ever. He'd been turned down for a vasectomy by three different specialists so far, due to his age, but as soon as he hit thirty-five, he wasn't taking no for an answer. It was one of the few ways for him to get back at Giaco, who'd tried hard to convince him to return to Chicago as his legally adopted heir so the family name could live on.

Ryan didn't have a real name of his own anymore, thanks to the Jackal, so he'd felt no need to oblige him. He'd once been Giaco Cienetti Tosaro, but that boy had died along with his father. He was a liar and a reformed thief. He could be a harsh businessman when left unchecked. He didn't have anything to offer any offspring that they could be proud of, in fact. Money was about all he had going for him, and even that wasn't a real attraction when one knew its source.

He had no idea what Elizabeth's expectations of a man might be, although he suspected they'd be high. It might be best for him to back off, at least until her probationary period was over. He couldn't very well tell her she wasn't right for the job after he'd kissed her—he didn't doubt for one minute that she'd take legal action against him if he tried. She had tons of spirit packed into that tiny frame. He admired that about her.

The pattering raindrops increased their tempo. Any second now, the sky would bust open. He straightened. The urge to kiss her wasn't gone, but it was under control.

"Go on and have breakfast before you get wet," he said. "I've got something to take care of in my office."

Chapter Six

Elizabeth

E LIZABETH WATCHED RYAN disappear up the path to the house. Mixed emotions abounded. She should have known better than to toss him like that again, but she'd gotten enormous satisfaction out of it, and it served him right.

For a few seconds, she'd thought he might kiss her in retaliation for it. She wouldn't have been surprised, since he'd been pretty free with his hands in the past when he thought she needed a lesson.

Her behavior was as inappropriate as his, she conceded, considering he was her boss and she was a female employee. If they were going to work together, they couldn't continue to carry on in this manner, no matter how much they rubbed each other the wrong way. The informality of the ranch environment was no excuse for a lack of professionalism on either of their parts. Obviously, he'd come to that realization first. Still, she couldn't help but wonder what might have happened if he had kissed her.

She trudged to the cookhouse, the shafts of her rubber boots slapping each other. Buckets of water upended and poured from the sky just as she opened the cookhouse door and darted inside. She picked up a tray and headed for the buffet.

"Is the weather in this state always so extreme?" she shouted to Steve, who was in charge of cooking bacon on the other side of the buffet counter. The rain thundering against the steel-clad roof made normal conversation almost impossible.

"What—you mean this little shower?" he shouted back.

Elizabeth took that as a yes.

The rain had eased up by the time she finished her breakfast. She dashed to her bunkhouse between downpours so she could shower and change her clothes before she had to be in her office at nine.

She found the note straightaway. Someone had stuck a folded sheet of lined loose leaf to the door, under the overhang, out of the rain.

She didn't think anything of it at first. Her mind had reverted to Ryan and her worry over how to get their relationship back on a professional track. Then it flipped to what she planned to wear, since the day was so wet and dreary. Leggings and a tunic would do. She dropped the note on the wooden table underneath the front room window where she liked to drink her first cup of coffee every morning before heading to work.

She'd showered, dressed, and was sipping black gold before she remembered the note. She opened it.

I think you're pretty.

Well, wasn't that nice.

A tiny ball of ice wedged in her chest. She stared at the note for long moments, trying to decide what to do, or if it warranted her doing anything at all. She wasn't comfortable with receiving the anonymous note, no. She especially didn't like the thought of one of the boys hanging around her living quarters, but since the ranch was a wide-open, communal space where everyone roamed as they pleased, there wasn't much she could say. To flag the path between the bunkhouses and the ranch house as her personal space would come across as extreme.

The real question was whether or not she should tell Ryan about it. He had a tendency to overreact when it came to women in jeopardy—whether real or imagined—and she didn't believe it was because she was special. She didn't want to give him an excuse to terminate her employment.

She finished her coffee, her morning routine on its head. She tucked the note in a pocket and locked the bunkhouse door behind her. It had started to rain again, although not as aggressively as before, but she was glad she'd opted for a flat-heeled pair of boots. The gravel path to the ranch house had turned into a stream.

She was hanging her coat at the main entry as Jazz

emerged from Dan's suite.

Elizabeth had a strong admiration for Jasmine 'Jazz' O'Reilly. Not only was she traffic-stoppingly beautiful, with long, muscular limbs, long-lashed blue eyes, and short, spiky blond hair, she had a job that commanded respect, too. She ran the smoke jumping and emergency services at the Custer County Airport. Elizabeth felt like a Smurf when she stood next to her.

"Hi, Elizabeth. How do you like working at the Endeavour so far?" Jazz asked cheerfully in a smoky, lounge singer voice that Elizabeth envied her almost as much as her height.

"So far, I love it." Except for that note. But she'd come into this job with her eyes open, and the incident would end up in her research, so there was that.

"Have you gone riding yet?"

"Afraid not. I don't know how," Elizabeth admitted.

"You'll learn. I'm not good at it either, but I enjoy it. It's a great way to see the ranch."

She doubted there was anything Jazz did that she wasn't good at. The woman was hardwired for success.

"I've got to get to the base," Jazz continued, zipping up a bright yellow slicker that enhanced the vivid blue of her eyes, "but we'll get a chance to chat more on Saturday night."

Ryan had a movie night planned. Trying to pick out one movie for four boys and eight adults was going to take trial and error. Elizabeth had suggested Japanese anime, to his complete and utter horror, a reaction she'd expected. One of the boys was deep into role-playing games and would likely appreciate anime, but everyone else would be lost. She'd then suggested the boys drop movie titles into a box and they'd draw from it each week. He'd been far more receptive to that.

"We're going to get either porn or movies with a lot of violence," Ryan warned her, as if she hadn't figured that out for herself.

"There's a simple solution," she replied. "For every inappropriate title we draw, we substitute a Hallmark movie from the women's network. Or maybe a children's cartoon. They're a captive audience. They'll get tired of that game pretty quick."

"That's evil," Ryan said. "I like it."

She saw Jazz off at the door, then straightened her shoulders. Ryan was in his office. She might as well tell him about the note now. If she left it too long it became a big deal, and she didn't want that.

His phone rang before she could reach his office, so she veered away and entered her own. She tried to speak to him several more times throughout the morning, but between the group home, the ranch, and some new rodeo venture, he was constantly either on the phone or in motion.

At three o'clock his office fell silent, but his door remained closed. She could see him through the glass wall panel, but he was engrossed in his work and didn't notice her. She was about to knock anyway when a newcomer entered the central lounge.

He dropped a bag on one of the leather sofas and sat down beside it, and checked his watch as if waiting for an appointment. He looked vaguely familiar, although she couldn't place him until he turned to her and she saw both sides of his face. His left cheek was a mass of scar tissue that puckered the skin and drew the corner of his mouth slightly off-center.

She didn't follow professional bull riding, but Miles Decker's story had been all over national news for days as people waited for word on his recovery. A former professional bull rider, he'd been working as the PBR spokesman until a tragic accident during a photo shoot had resulted in his being gored by a bull. Its horn had hooked on Miles's left shoulder, then gouged his left cheek from his chin to his temple. The scar, while disfiguring, wasn't the worst thing that could have happened. He'd been lucky he wasn't blinded or killed.

And the scar wasn't what had her staring. He owned the self-assurance of a man who didn't give a damn how he looked on the surface because he knew he was still hotter than most men alive. He left her a little weak in the knees, too. It was hard not to admire the depth and breadth of his self-confidence.

He took off his hat and settled it on his knee. "Miles Decker," he said, introducing himself with an accompanying bob of his chin while keeping his eyes locked steady on hers.

Montana men had a unique blend of politeness, modesty, and seduction in their manners that proved fairly potent. Their mothers had raised these men right. "I'm here to see Ryan O'Connell. I have an appointment for three."

It was on the tip of Elizabeth's tongue to explain she wasn't Ryan's administrative assistant, then asked herself what difference it could possibly make when she was standing right outside his office. "I'll let him know."

She knocked on his door and poked her head in.

He'd unbuttoned his collar and rolled up his sleeves. He wore a smudge of grease on one corded forearm. He'd been in and out of the office all day and the machine shed must have been one of his stops. Her breath raked against her ribs. She'd never met two men less alike, and yet, they elicited the exact same response from a woman. Miles Decker knew he was hot. Ryan, on the other hand, hadn't a clue that the whole dark, mysterious, and brooding image worked equally well in his favor. Some women went nuts over that look.

She did too. A little. Her poor father would flip.

"Your three o'clock appointment is here, Mr. O'Connell," she said brightly.

Confusion colored Ryan's expression. "What the..." he began, hopefully mystified by being called *mister* and not from reading the direction her thoughts had taken. Then his gaze drifted past her shoulder, he saw he had a visitor, and the lightbulb blinked on. Amusement flirted with the grim angles of his mouth. "Thank you, Elizabeth, that will be all.

Hold my calls for the next hour. Oh, and would you mind bringing us coffee?"

"Not at all." She'd squeeze it in between her conference call with the local high school guidance counselor and prepping for upcoming counseling sessions.

A few minutes later, she stood in front of the burbling coffeepot, wondering how far she should push this. How good was Heathcliff's sense of humor?

She loaded a tray with two heavy white porcelain mugs of coffee, a tiny pitcher of cream, and a matching bowl of sugar. She carried the tray to Ryan's office and carefully placed it on his desk. She lifted one of the mugs and passed it to him without comment, but met his eyes with a silent challenge in hers. *Go ahead and drink it. I dare you.*

Ryan considered the mug with suspicion for a long moment. He set it down. "Miles, I'd like you to meet Elizabeth Benson. She's the case manager for the Endeavour's group home and in charge of its programming. Elizabeth, Miles will be running the Endeavour's new circuit rodeo."

Miles offered her his hand along with a slow, sensual smile that drew a woman's eyes from his ruined cheek to a pair of very promising lips. He was, as her grandmother liked to say, completely and utterly *sex on a stick.* "Pleased to meet you, Elizabeth."

"Likewise."

Ryan donned his dour, Heathcliff persona. The dark look he telegraphed her read, *"Don't you have your own work to do?"*

She took the hint. This was a business, after all. "Enjoy your coffee, gentlemen," she said, injecting extra cheerfulness into her tone. She let her gaze drift Miles's way. Heathcliff should take a few lessons on the right way to attract a woman's attention. Miles was a natural flirt and there was no harm in flirting back.

"I'll be right next door if you need me for anything." She remembered why she'd been trying to corner Ryan all day. She fished the note from her pocket and passed it to him. "When you get a few moments, I'd like to speak to you about this."

She returned to her office and closed the door so she could take that conference call with the school in private, smugly satisfied with herself. She wondered how long it would take Ryan to discover she hadn't done a thing to his coffee.

Ryan

RYAN TUCKED THE piece of paper under his day planner to deal with later. Right now, he was more preoccupied with the hiring mistakes he'd been making of late. First Elizabeth, who Miles hadn't taken his eyes off, and now Miles—because Elizabeth had responded to him in kind. She'd acted as if she'd never seen a cowboy, before.

Was she going to create a problem for him with every male on the ranch?

"That's who is in charge of a group of delinquent teen-aged boys?" Miles asked. The twist of his mouth and the doubt in his tone conveyed the same opinion Ryan held on the matter—*only an idiot would ever think that will go well.*

"Looks can be deceiving," he said, because while no, he didn't believe it would work either, he also discovered he didn't like having anyone think Elizabeth wasn't competent. "Elizabeth is a licensed professional with a master's degree in social work and a great deal of practical experience. She can take care of herself." The cooling mug of coffee caught his eye. *Exhibit A.* No way was he touching that.

"If you say so."

"The Endeavour has a code of conduct with regard to staff fraternization," Ryan added, because he hadn't liked the way Miles and Elizabeth looked at each other. Miles had bought a house in Grand, for which Ryan was now thankful, although he'd be assigned quarters on the ranch for his personal use, too. "It's informal right now, but we'll be firming it up over the next couple of weeks."

"I see." Miles cocked his head, frowning as if this infor-mation required serious and deep consideration, and might well be a deal breaker. "How many women are on staff?"

"So far, just Elizabeth," Ryan said grudgingly, because admitting it made it sound as if the code of conduct had been something he'd come up with on the spur of the moment, which it was. It also sounded as if he were warning Miles off—also true. And he wasn't the least bit comfortable with that particular discovery, either. "But once the rodeo is up and running, we'll have room on staff for more women. The Endeavour is an equal opportunity employer." He could already hear Dan laughing over that particular statement. *Since when?*

Since Dan was the one who insisted he give Elizabeth a chance, making everything his fault. That was when.

He and Miles spent the next hour discussing plans for the rodeo and how to keep it competitive in a difficult market. It would take place over a full week. They'd start off the first day with horse races, followed by a bull auction, another event Ryan had his eye on as part of a long-term business plan. There would also need to be live entertainment each evening. And, of course, they'd have bull and bronc riding, as well as barrel racing, competitions.

After Miles left, Ryan spent a few quiet moments considering the untouched mug of coffee. He picked it up and sniffed it. Then, he took a cautious sip. He tasted nothing but cold coffee.

She was good.

The slip of paper he'd stuck under his day planner caught his attention. He unfolded it.

I think you're pretty.

He folded it again, smoothed it carefully, then placed it

in a drawer out of sight. He tapped his fingers on his desk and stared at the framed photo on the wall of him with Dan and Dallas, arms around each other's shoulders, grinning like fools. The photo was from a corporate retreat disguised as a fishing trip.

He'd taken a big risk by drawing them into his grandfather's money, but he'd wanted to make their lives easier. He'd wanted to help make their dreams come true. He'd also been terrified of handling all that money alone, without any purpose for it.

If they ever found out the true source of the money, their friendship might well be ruined. He'd been willing to gamble because the risk had been worth it. Besides, the chances of them finding out were so small as to be next to impossible.

He wasn't willing to gamble with Elizabeth's well-being, however. Therefore, she'd be on the next flight home to Chicago.

She was on the phone when he entered her office. She held up one finger and waved him into a chair. He waited while she finished a conversation with the public school over the enrollment of two of the boys, Angel and Paisley. Paisley was one of the next boys to arrive.

"Sure. Let's send the two sex offenders to the local high school," Ryan said when she got off the phone. "That will make us popular with the parents in Grand."

Elizabeth's long, dark-red curls shrouded her shoulders. She'd dressed in her version of casual today, meaning she

looked young and fresh and appealing—all of which translated to vulnerable, as far as he was concerned. *"Looks can be
deceiving."*

He'd actually said that to Miles.

What bullshit.

"Angel isn't a sex offender," she said calmly. "By law, and
according to the information I have on file, he's a victim.
The guidance counselor at Grand High is aware there might
be more to his story. And Paisley had a relationship with a
sexually aware twelve-year-old girl who's admitted she told
him she was sixteen. So, while technically he is considered a
sex offender, in reality, he's also a teenager who is immature
for his age, and whose real crime is poor judgment."

Ryan got all of that. His major concern was which of the
exhibitors of poor judgment in residence was responsible for
the note in his desk drawer.

"Let's talk about that note for a moment, shall we?" he
said. "I assume you didn't give it to me because you think
I'm pretty."

Amber eyes gave him a frank and decidedly nonclinical
examination that left him feeling... bothered. How did she
always manage to get under his skin?

"I would never have used the word pretty to describe
you," she said when she was done. Her smile was sweet. "By
the way—how was your coffee?"

"Cold," he said sourly.

"Odd. It was hot when I gave it to you."

He'd like to give her something hot…

He had to get rid of her. Now. "Let's get back to the note."

"Let's put it in perspective," she countered. "You've got a group of misfit teenaged boys with rampaging hormones and terrible judgment stuck on an isolated ranch with one woman on staff. After all, I am pretty, you've got to admit." Her eyes dared him to argue.

"You aren't exactly helping your case for why I shouldn't send you packing tonight," Ryan replied, ignoring the taunt, because while yes, she was pretty—the understatement of the year, by the way—he was no teenaged boy, and taunting him might not be in her best interests.

"Yes, I am," she rattled on, blithely unaware that the current danger sat directly in front of her. "I thought you might overreact, which is why I brought it to your attention immediately. I won't keep information involving the boys from you, Ryan. At the end of the day, as pretty as I am, I'm not a teenaged girl, I'm a woman, and I'm not about to instigate an affair with a boy. There's no real harm in a note as long as there's no escalation. We should come up with a professional and appropriate response if there is."

"I'm not overreacting."

Elizabeth's lips pressed into a firm line. "Honestly, is that your takeaway from what I just said? For your information, threatening to send me packing over one little note from a troubled boy, when troubled boys are the whole reason I'm here, is a definite overreaction."

When she put it like that... "If you gave them the same stink eye you're giving me right now, any inappropriate thoughts they might have about you are going to shrivel and die."

"Exactly. I'm a professional, not a naïve girl. I will admit, however, that I don't like the idea of an anonymous someone having access to my private living space. I prefer to know who—and what—I'm dealing with. You said you have security cameras set up around the ranch. Do you have one outside my bunkhouse?"

"Yes." The cameras only stored footage for a week, but the note had been placed there this morning. He would have remembered it if she hadn't gone out of her way to upend him. "I'll look into it."

"Thank you."

She acted as if the whole matter were settled when they had barely begun to address the many issues he had. Sending her home might not be an option just yet, but neither was he about to let the hot little fairy continue to run free, wreaking havoc. Young John and Handy spent way too much time in the barns when she was feeding the orphans. Miles Decker looked at her as if she were a prized bull and he was about to get the ride of his life. And now one of the kids was leaving her love notes.

This wasn't at all what he'd envisioned for the Endeavour group home. He'd pictured camping trips. Horseback riding. Hard work to wear the boys out and plenty of fresh air to help them fall asleep. All of the things that would have helped him as a teen, but he hadn't found until he was in college. Not until after he met Dan and Dallas and began spending summers with them.

"We're not done here," he said. For once, she was going to listen to him. "I don't like the idea of anyone on this ranch having access to your private living space either, especially not when you're in it all by yourself, but I have a solution. This house is huge. I have an entire guest suite at my disposal and you're the only person who's ever used it. Until we hire more female staff to share the bunkhouse with you, the guest suite is yours."

"I don't think so," she said, chin up, eyes calm, message clear.

Make me.

Chapter Seven

Elizabeth

S IX EXTRA-LARGE, EMPTY pizza boxes, along with paper plates and soda cans, littered the floor of the lounge. Elizabeth forged a path through the detritus while carrying two enormous bowls of popcorn. Ryan, behind her, carried two more.

It was movie night. The feature film was Disney's *Frozen*, because as expected, the first movie Ryan had drawn from the suggestion box had been excessively violent. He'd countered with *How to Train Your Dragon*, but Elizabeth had argued the boys might not learn enough of a lesson from that and a Disney princess would be far more effective.

They set three bowls of popcorn on folding tables within easy reach of the teens. Elizabeth passed the fourth bowl to Dan.

Bean bag chairs had been brought in for the boys. Four leather sofas had been reserved for the adults. The counselors, Colin and Ace, took one of the sofas. Dan and Jazz had one to themselves, as did Dallas and Hannah, who were snuggled up adorably close. That left one sofa for Elizabeth and Ryan to share, which was unfortunate, because matters remained somewhat tense between them.

He hadn't liked that she'd turned down the use of his guest suite, but living so close to her angsty, dominating, but undeniably attractive boss had danger written all over it. She knew a difficult man when she saw one and he nailed the profile. If his closely guarded background hadn't already raised a red flag, his micromanagement tendencies would have shaken it under her nose. Combined, they indicated significant issues with trust. And as for his dominance issues...

If a woman ever allowed him to make decisions for her, he'd quickly take over her life. In that regard, he was a little too much like her father. She'd barely distanced herself from a similar overprotective situation and wasn't anxious to plunge into another.

She also understood the value of keeping her professional and private lives separate—as much as possible, since she lived at the ranch twenty-four seven—for the sake of her mental health. Helping people cope with their problems meant keeping her own to a minimum.

But, even after taking all that into consideration, once she'd found out Jonas was the one who'd left her the note, she'd come close to changing her mind. While her file on him didn't contain nearly as much information as what Ryan had supplied, all of it combined was enough to sound an alarm. His background read a little too much like that of the boy who'd killed Marianne for her to feel comfortable.

The bias was hers. In the few interactions they'd had, Jonas came across as friendly and highly charismatic. He'd shown no evidence of violent tendencies toward people or animals, and as far as she could tell, from the information made available to her, he'd never had a serious girlfriend.

But the jealousy and obsession were there. He'd bashed in the windshield of a friend's car because the friend had won a position on the school varsity football team and he hadn't. He'd burned down his parents' garage—including a Mercedes and a brand-new Audi—after they'd taken away his driving privileges over a speeding ticket. Ryan had turned up that last detail on his own because the parents hadn't filed an insurance claim. That omission, in itself, indicated trouble at home. They'd tried to cover up their son's bad behavior and that was never a healthy reaction.

Plus, underneath the charisma, Jonas was arrogant and entitled. He'd gotten into a fistfight with Tyce and had to be moved to a different bunkhouse—although in fairness to Jonas, Tyce took offense easily and would drop the gloves over any perceived slight.

So, she hadn't ruled out Ryan's guest suite completely. She simply hadn't decided whether or not she'd be moving from one difficult situation to another.

"Why do we have to watch a girl movie?" someone complained.

"What's the matter? Don't you like girls?" Jazz, who dealt with men behaving like boys every day, and appeared indifferent to the concept of political correctness, inquired.

The boy's name was Owen and his cheeks took on the hue of a ripened tomato. Jazz was so pretty and athletic, and owned such a commanding presence, that the boys were completely intimidated by her. "I like big girls. I don't like little girl movies."

Jazz scooped up a handful of popcorn and tossed a popped kernel into her mouth. "You have three big girls sitting right here who do like this movie, so maybe you should use this as an opportunity to find out what we like about it. The information might come in handy someday."

"I like the music," Hannah chimed in, dimples flashing.

Hannah was another imposing giantess, at least by height-challenged Elizabeth's standards. While equally as pretty as Jazz, she had such a kind, warm personality that her looks were usually the second thing anyone noticed. She was one of those people everyone liked and naturally gravitated toward, and teenaged boys proved no exception. She'd told Elizabeth she had two brothers, and since Dallas had three, each in their early twenties, she, too, was comfortable around rampaging testosterone.

"I'm only here to humor the women," Dallas added. "I voted for *Dead Pool*."

Elizabeth turned a laugh into a cough. Now they knew where tonight's original movie suggestion had come from.

Shaggy-haired Dallas was sweet, and from what she'd heard an excellent doctor, but also that he wasn't especially adept at reading a room.

"You and I need to talk," Ryan said to him.

"What about?" Dallas asked, furthering his reputation for obliviousness.

Dan, stretched out on the sofa, had his arm draped around Jazz. "Don't mind me. I'm here to shoot anyone who tries to leave early."

Ryan and Elizabeth took their seats. The sofa was comfortable, but deep enough that she had to tuck her legs under her so they didn't dangle above the floor like a child's. Ryan sprawled next to her, taking up two-thirds of their shared space because he didn't suffer from the same size affliction. Her toes brushed against a solid thigh—provoking a reaction that proved keeping her professional and private lives separate was going to be difficult enough without her moving into his guest room.

Ryan took command of the remote.

"I don't think I'll need to worry about getting any more notes telling me I'm pretty after tonight," she leaned over and murmured to him as the movie began.

"What makes you say that?"

"Two gorgeous supermodels eclipse one cute little person."

Black pupils expanded, swallowing cocoa irises flecked with gold. He let out a low chuckle and dipped his head close to her ear, speaking under cover of the opening credits. His warm breath brushed the side of her throat. "For all of your education and training, you can be kind of stupid."

"*Hey.* Will that assessment be on my six-month performance appraisal?" she whispered back, hoping to provoke another laugh out of him. When he laughed, Heathcliff vanished, making it more understandable as to why Dallas and Dan, both so much friendlier and far more outgoing, were such loyal friends.

Instead, he turned his head toward the ten-foot theater screen mounted on the wall and the moment was broken. "Watch the movie, Elizabeth. You picked it out."

The movie was one hundred and two minutes of torture for the fifteen males present. After it finished streaming and satellite TV came on, one of the counselors seized the remote and flipped to a documentary channel. *The Day of the Jackal: The Mystery Surrounding One of Chicago's Greatest Crime Families* was featured.

So many stories about Chicago's crime families floated around that it was hard to sort fact from fiction. Elizabeth had heard several versions of this particular one, but the probable truth to it was that Giaco "the Jackal" Cienetti's only daughter and her family had faded from the public eye years ago, not liking the notoriety surrounding her infamous father.

"This is more like it," Jonas said.

Ryan seized the remote and switched to BBC Earth.

"Let's try something more educational. A mind is a terrible thing to waste."

"If it's such a waste, why did we spend almost two hours watching a little kid movie?" Owen, the fourth boy in residence, asked.

Ace, who claimed he'd been named after Ace Ventura because his mom was a Jim Carrey fan, tapped his young charge on the top of the head. "The movie was to open your mind. Education is to expand it. Be quiet and pay attention, young grasshopper."

An aerial tour of the Nile proved to be exactly what everyone needed to bore them to sleep.

"Movie night sucks," Owen said when the program was over.

"Imagine how much more fun it would be from the local jail," Dan replied. "Next Saturday night you can sit there for five hours, if you'd like to find out for yourself."

Owen might be quiet, but he had plenty of nerve. "I'll think about it," he said.

The counselors helped the boys pick up their trash and sort it into bags, then shepherded them back to the bunkhouses while the remaining adults put the furniture back where it belonged.

With order restored, Dan and Jazz, then Dallas and Hannah, disappeared into their respective apartments.

Elizabeth carried empty popcorn bowls to Ryan's kitchen and came nose to chest with him on her return trip to the lounge. It wasn't that he was exceptionally tall, although he was above average height—she'd worn ballet flats because her normal high heels would have come across as ridiculous when paired with her jeans.

She couldn't stand and stare at him all night. It was past midnight. They both had early starts in the morning. The orphans didn't feed themselves and it was too late to change shifts with one of the hands.

"See you tomorrow," she said, attempting to dodge around him, but he blocked the door from his suite to the lounge.

"I'll walk you to your bunkhouse. It's dark outside," he said.

"It's less than one hundred yards away and the path is lit. I can't possibly get lost."

"I'm not worried about you getting lost."

While she didn't like to admit it out loud because she knew it was silly, his company would be welcome. She was a city girl, more afraid of raccoons, bears, and the multitude of foreign night noises than a misguided teenager most likely already asleep, so she might as well give in and be gracious.

"Thank you. It's kind of you to offer," she said.

"I'm not being kind, either."

And... Heathcliff was back. She sighed. She had no idea what she was supposed to make out of that comment, so she didn't try.

"I'll get my sweater," she said.

Ryan

HE WASN'T KIND. Especially not where Elizabeth was concerned.

He was often too blunt with her. She left him restless and on edge. Unable to focus. She was like a burr under a saddle. A tooth in need of extraction. Movie night, with her next to him, and him hyperaware of her presence for five hours, had been a fresh form of hell.

Showing her kindness would only escalate the level of aggravation and worry she caused him. If he could find a way to be rid of her before her six months were up, maybe he'd sleep better at night.

But letting her walk to her empty bunkhouse alone after dark was not going to happen. If she'd moved into the guest suite, like he wanted, life would be easier for him.

He held her sweater for her while she eased her arms into the sleeves. A long lock of curly red hair slid over his wrist. His lungs drew in the soft, feminine scent of her skin, then filtered it into his blood to spread heat throughout his entire body. Yet another source of irritation she caused him.

He opened the door, letting the fresh air clear his head. "After you."

The night, when they stepped into it, swallowed them up. A sliver of pale-yellow moon cut into a bottomless, star-spangled sky. Although May, the air cooled considerably after sundown. A string of ground-level solar lights lit the shadowy path to the bunkhouses.

They walked side-by-side, their shoes crunching on gravel. Something rustled in the neatly trimmed grass a few feet away. A mechanical churring, followed by a series of chirps, had Elizabeth scrabbling for his arm.

"Is that a snake?"

She pressed up against him, proving she had terrible instincts as far as self-preservation went. If she knew the thoughts he had in his head about her right now, she'd run away screaming, instead.

"No. It's a nightjar—a small nighthawk. It's hunting bugs."

"Sorry for being so jumpy," she said. "I expected it to be quiet in the country at night, but it's almost as loud as the city. Just in a different way. I'm not used to it yet."

He'd never considered the possibility that she might be frightened by the sounds the ranch made at night. He hadn't forgotten what it was like to lie awake in the dark, listening for footsteps, afraid the bad guys might find him—although the move to Montana had dulled those fears for him.

A comforting hug—the kind Dallie might offer in this situation—was beyond him, however. He was as skittish of her as she was of snakes, and under normal conditions, he made every effort to avoid physical contact with either. Awkwardly patting the hand with the death grip on his arm was the best he had in him.

"I can identify most of the noises for you, if you want," he heard himself offer. He stopped in the middle of the path. "Listen for a sec. Then, tell me what you think you hear."

She tilted her head as she focused. The night tightened around them. The sliver of moon and the ground-level solar lighting limned the delicate lines of her face. She crinkled her nose. "I hear a disorganized orchestra led by a conductor gone mad."

That made him smile. "I've never heard spring peepers described quite that way, before." He'd always found their song peaceful. "You're going to have to be more open-minded than that."

"If you say so." Little by little, she began to parse out different sounds. "I hear the river."

"That was too easy." The Tongue River flowed alongside the Endeavour Ranch, meeting the Yellowstone River on the far side of Grand. "Be more specific," he urged her. "Water makes a particular trickling sound as it flows over rocks—light, but steady. Can you hear it?" She closed her eyes, listened, then nodded. "There are lots of sounds to choose from. Pick one out and think about what might make it—is it the wind, the water, or an animal?"

She stood like she was crafted of stone, not opening her eyes. "I hear the branches of the trees rubbing together. Wind. I hear the leaves rustling. Also wind." She waited, intent on something new. Less obvious. "I hear a clicking.

Animal?"

He heard the clicking, too. "Yes. Bird," he clarified. "It's nesting season. It's a pair of great blue herons snapping their bill tips together."

A loud splash came from the Tongue. Her fingers bit into his arm.

"What was that? Animal," she added hastily.

"Pretty sure that was a beaver slapping its tail on the water. Something likely got a little too close so it sounded a warning." He made a mental note to send someone down to make sure the pests weren't flooding the fields, although he didn't say that to her. She might ask questions with answers a city girl wouldn't much care for.

"It's so beautiful here," she breathed, lifting her face. Her wide eyes absorbed the faint trickle of moonlight. "Thank you for showing me how to appreciate it."

He wished she didn't look so damned appealing. Certainty churned in his gut—she wasn't going to leave when her six months of probation were up. She wouldn't give him cause to dismiss her, either. What was he going to do about it? How was he supposed to deal with her, day in and day out, when she drove him to distraction? How could he ignore the temptation she presented?

Self-restraint wasn't part of his nature. His mother might have chosen a new name for him, but deep down, he was a Tosaro and a Cienetti—greedy and ruthless and ready to take whatever he wanted. His grand theft auto days were proof enough of that. So was his willingness to accept his grandfather's money and lie to his friends.

He brought his palm to her cheek, rubbing the blunt of his thumb along the slender line of her throat. He bent his head over hers. "You have to the count of five to tell me you don't want me to kiss you," he said, the words scratching his throat, making them raspy and harsh.

Then, on the count of three, he captured her upturned lips with his. Elizabeth absorbed all his senses. The clicking, the peepers, the rustling of the wind... It all disappeared. Instead, he heard the catch of her breath. Felt the slight tremble of her small frame against his. Tasted the warm, sugar sweetness of her mouth. In his head, he envisioned her naked, in his bed, while his hands explored every inch of her ivory skin.

That vivid mental image, tempting as it was, brought his common sense back into play. He lifted his head and dropped his hands to his sides, acutely and painfully aware he'd just made their workplace that much more intense.

He tried to make light of it, even though he'd been profoundly unsettled. "This is where you're supposed to toss me on my ass and break one of my legs."

"Over a kiss?" Her light laugh dispelled any worry that he might have unsettled her, too. "If I were going to break your leg for anything, it would have been when you groped me."

"When I did *what?*" He stared at her, his brain a complete blank as he racked through it, trying to sift out what she referred to. Then, he had it. Her teambuilding session the day she'd arrived. He'd been so intent on showing her the flaw in her self-defense display that he hadn't considered how it might be construed. "I didn't grope you. I was proving that in a real-life situation, an attacker isn't going to play fair."

"Po-tay-to, po-tah-to," she said with a sniff. "Groping me deserves a broken leg. Kissing me doesn't, even though apparently, you can't count to five. But I am curious as to why you did kiss me," she added, sounding interested on a purely clinical level, which he found damned insulting.

Social workers were the worst. She wanted him to explain, which in itself was no big shock, considering how many therapists and social workers he'd dealt with during his misspent teen years. They were always asking for explanations, and more often than not, he'd had none to give them.

This time he did. He'd kissed her for the same reason he'd once stolen cars. She was beautiful and sleek and untouchable, and he longed to possess her for the high it would give him.

But he sure as hell wasn't going to give those reasons to her. "Move it along, city girl. We don't have all night. There's work to be done in the morning and the animals won't wait."

She fell in beside him, surprisingly quiet, to his intense relief. He hadn't expected her to give up her line of questioning quite so easily.

She'd left the outside light on at the bunkhouse. They reached the front steps. She paused with one foot on the first stair tread and turned.

"You didn't answer my question," she said.

She wasn't going to let it go, after all. Her expression was impossible for him to interpret. His stomach bounced off his ribs. He thrust his hands in his jacket pockets. "Curiosity, mostly. I wanted to see how you'd react." Then, because he'd never liked being put on the defensive, he raised a question of his own. "A better one might be, why did you let me?"

Her smile, honest and wide, shone from her eyes. "Because I wanted you to."

She skipped up the three remaining steps to the veranda, unlocked the door, and had it opened and closed behind her, leaving him standing outside alone, trying to figure out what had just happened.

Chapter Eight

Elizabeth

ELIZABETH DIDN'T TURN on any inside lights. She leaned against the door, pressing her hands and her ear against the cool wooden panel, and focused on taking deep, normal breaths, allowing her overtaxed lungs to decompress while she waited for Ryan's next move.

Because I wanted you to.

She shouldn't have said that.

All was quiet outside at first. Then, footsteps chewed into gravel. Her pounding heart slowed in correlation to the sound of footsteps fading into the night.

She closed her eyes. It had been a long time since she'd been this aware of a man. Maybe never. Worse, there was interest on both their parts, not only hers, which was going to make it twice as hard for her to ignore.

And she should ignore it. Sexually, they were far too aware of each other for an employer-employee relationship. He was such a fascinating blend of restraint and feral need. He kissed as if the world were about to end and they were the last two people left in it alive.

But she didn't lie to herself and pretend there was anything more to it than that. She knew what the drawbacks would be. He could no more give up control of a relationship than he could hand over the reins of the ranch. When things ended—which they would, because his weren't terms she'd ever accept—she'd be the one who'd have to leave.

She heard light footsteps cross the veranda. She assumed it must be him, returning to tell her not to read too much into that kiss. Otherwise, it might be wise to start planning her exit strategy now.

When she opened the door she found Jonas, about to place a small bouquet of spring flowers on the stoop. He stared up at her with a deer-in-the-headlights look in his eyes. It was hard to say which one of them was the more surprised.

She recovered first. "Aren't you supposed to be in bed?"

Jonas glanced up the dimly lit path to the house. "I figured you would be, too."

She didn't like his knowing smile and what it inferred. She wondered if he'd seen her with Ryan, but it might be best not to wonder about that too much. Her takeaway was that not much remained private on the ranch and she'd do well to remember that in the future.

The best way to claim control of this situation was to treat it lightly, while at the same time, exerting authority. "Then why are you here?"

Jonas recovered the cheekiness only teenagers seemed able to pull off. "Angel dared me."

That was a plausible enough explanation that she was willing to accept as long as it got him off her doorstep. "I guess you showed him," she said. "If he needs confirmation that you followed through, you can send him to me. In the future, however, when your counselor says it's lights out, he means for you to be in your bunk." She began to close the door. "Good night."

Jonas thrust one hand out to stop it before it could latch. He pushed it wider and held out the yellow buttercups and pink shooting stars. "Here. These are for you."

She didn't like the vibe she was getting. She didn't like the way he tried to see past the door and into her home, and she wished she'd turned on the lights. She definitely didn't like that he'd muscled the door open, proving how much stronger he was than her, even though he was undersized for his age.

There was also a strong possibility she wasn't as ready to work with teenaged boys as she'd believed, despite all her formal education. Ryan was right. She was stupid. Theory was one thing. Practice, another entirely.

"Thank you," she said coolly, falling back on her education, because that was the best defensive weapon she had. "I'll accept them this once, but it's inappropriate for you to be bringing me gifts of any kind and I won't accept them again."

She debated telling him to stay away from her private living quarters too, because that worried her a lot more than the note or the flowers, then decided against it. She'd leave that to his counselor when she spoke to him about this tomorrow. The goal right now was to de-escalate, not cause direct confrontation.

"Could I get a drink of water?" he asked.

He'd blocked the doorway. He inched a little farther into the room, forcing her to take a step back, making her more conscious of the fact the room behind her was in darkness.

Intellectually, she understood he had a poor grasp of socially acceptable behavior—he wasn't at the ranch because he fit so well into society. But, while his intentions might be harmless enough, they might also not be, and the situation had progressed beyond her ability to control it.

Was this what had happened to her sister? Had she believed no real harm was intended until it was too late? *Could I break this boy's leg?*

That last cold, practical thought flashed into her head as she assessed her next move.

Fortunately, the decision was taken out of her hands.

"There's water in your own bunkhouse. Go back to bed." Ryan's cold voice carried from partway up the path. Long strides carried him toward them with the implacable force of a train.

Despite Jonas's poor social skills, he seemed to understand self-preservation well enough. He didn't waste time on explanations or goodbyes, but jumped off the side of the veranda and disappeared into the shadows seconds before Ryan emerged into the light.

Waves of relief crashed over Elizabeth, leaving her knees about to collapse. She'd never been so glad to see him, even though this was no white-hatted, cowboy hero, swooping in to save the day. This was an angry black angel who looked ready to tear the whole world apart.

"Pack up what you need for tonight and the morning. I'll wait. Tomorrow, we'll move your belongings into the guest suite," he ordered her, sounding a lot more in control of himself than he looked.

If she'd had the night to think about it, she'd likely have found a reason for why she should stay put. As it was, she was concerned enough about his mental state that she had no interest in arguing with him—not simply for the sake of it. He was in no mood.

He bounded up the steps and pried the wilting flowers from her hand that she hadn't realized she still held. He flipped the interior light on and carried the flowers to the trash can beside the sink in the small kitchenette. The lid opened and closed with a bang. The frigid look in his dark eyes when he returned to the bunkroom eclipsed anything a mere, brooding Heathcliff could have conjured. It was truly frightening, although she wasn't afraid for herself.

"Jonas is just a boy," she began. "But—"

"I know what he is." Ryan's gaze thawed somewhat when

it settled on her, although it became no less wild and alarming. "He's an undersized kid trying to prove he's a big man by intimidating someone smaller and weaker than he is. He enjoys pushing people to their limits because he's never had to face consequences. He takes what he wants, and if for some reason he can't get it, he has to diminish or destroy it. He's an egomaniac with an inferiority complex who's just earned himself a month's worth of fencing. And don't bother telling me it's too heavy for him, or it might interfere with his schoolwork, because you'll be wasting your breath."

She didn't know much about fencing, but she did know it involved a lot of hard work and that the hired hands complained incessantly about it.

She also knew self-recrimination and guilt when she saw it. It blazed behind the ice in his eyes. In his head, worst-case scenarios were playing out as to what might have happened if he hadn't turned back.

The reason why he'd decided to turn back was a whole other matter.

She threw her arms around his waist and hugged him, pressing her forehead to his chest and the knitted softness of his jersey shirt beneath his partially unzipped jacket.

"I was going to say thank you," she said.

Ryan

A CUTE LITTLE person.

Right.

Elizabeth's arms closed around him. He folded his around her, mostly in an automatic response, because he'd entered uncharted territory as far as his interactions with women were concerned. The ones he normally pursued tended to be what polite people called worldly. They didn't particularly inspire this need to protect. Any one of them would have had that boy on his knees, doubled over in agony, cradling his damaged goods. For all Elizabeth's education, work experience, self-defense lessons, and talk, overprotective parents had left her idealistic and that translated to vulnerable.

"I'm fine. I just need a moment," she assured him, the warmth of her breath cutting into his skin.

The raging inferno inside him slowly burned itself out and he found himself talking. He didn't know why. Maybe he wanted to give her something different to focus on. Maybe he wanted her to know that he wasn't planning to kill Jonas, even though the little shit was lucky he hadn't kicked his ass all the way back to his bunkhouse. Maybe he needed to remind himself of why that would have been a really bad idea, because he'd been sorely tempted—but violence was his grandfather's approach to problem-solving and would never be his again.

"As a kid, maybe eleven or twelve, I used to get in fights almost every day," he said, absently rubbing the heel of one hand in a circular motion between Elizabeth's slender shoulders. God, she was fragile... The rage threatened to reemerge, so he tucked his chin into her crown of glossy red curls and talked faster. "It didn't matter how big the other kid was. The bigger, the better. Win or lose, I didn't care. My mom got to the point where she couldn't take it anymore, so she dumped me back into therapy. The therapist told me I had an unresolved need to take control of situations and not be a passive victim. She suggested I come up with a way to address that need other than resorting to violence. So I started stealing cars."

"I'm impressed you listened to her, although I'll assume she suggested a different sport—something like football or rugby. I would have recommended track and field if I were her, though. To minimize physical contact." Then, after she had him all twisted around so he wasn't sure where she was going with her train of thought, she asked, "Why were you in therapy in the first place?"

He hadn't seen that question coming. Served him right for opening up. He tried to decide how much history he was comfortable in revealing to her. It went with a high level of trust.

He did trust her, though. "This is in confidence, okay?"

She nodded her understanding.

Her calmness went a long way toward cooling his anger.

He spoke to the top of her head, glad she wasn't watching him, because he couldn't bring himself to tell her the whole story. He'd never told it to anyone—not therapists, not Dallas and Dan. Secrecy was what kept the Adriana Gallants of the world from his doorstep. His mother had drummed that message home.

The Day of the Jackal... What kind of lame-ass, unoriginal title for a fakeumentary was that?

"When I was seven, my father was murdered. I was in bed asleep, but I woke up when I heard noises downstairs. They didn't know I was there. I was supposed to be at my grandfather's, but my mom and I came home early. They were all in the front foyer and I watched it happen from the upstairs landing." And he watched it again and again in his nightmares, although only every few months now, as opposed to every night.

"Where was your mom during all this?"

She sounded like Dan, who turned everything into an interrogation. But he could feel her relax, so he didn't object. "Does it matter?"

"I think so, yes."

"She was in the foyer too, being restrained by two men."

He hadn't planned on getting this deep into the story. The memory of it made his chest hurt. Normally, whenever forced to confront it, he managed to separate himself enough to relay it as if it were a movie he'd watched. Talking to Elizabeth about it was different.

Her clasped hands tightened against the small of his back. She leaned back slightly to look up at him. "There were three attackers altogether, as well as your mother and father? Was it a robbery gone bad, or was your father the target?"

"And… this is now one of those conversations I wish I'd never started," Ryan said lightly, forcing humor into his words. It had happened so long ago, and to people who were now dead, that the grip it maintained on his life was nothing short of ridiculous. "It was a hit, okay? My dad wasn't one of the good guys."

"Which is why they weren't interested in your mother."

They'd been interested in her, alright. They'd hauled her off to his grandfather's—who had ordered the hit, as it turned out. He'd huddled in his bed with the lights out for hours, waiting for her to return. When she did, her face was swollen and bruised. Her lip split. He never learned what had happened to his father's body and he no longer wanted to know.

"She moved us to Montana soon after that," he said. He left out the part about the witness protection program. "I've been told that seeing the murder and being unable to do anything about it is why I have control issues. It's also the reason I don't go after anyone smaller or weaker than me, which is why I brought up this sordid story in the first place—if you're worried about what I might do to Jonas, don't be. I don't condone violence. I understand it, mind you. But we don't engage in corporal punishment here. I provide the facilities, recreation, and program funding for the group home. Any therapy is up to the case manager and counselors. Handy will take charge of him while he's fencing."

Elizabeth seized on a detail he hadn't intended. "Why would your mother move you to Montana?"

"Probably because it's about as far from Chicago as you can get in this country, at least in terms of lifestyle." Plus, no one would ever have thought to search for his glamorous, socialite mother here. Sadly, they were right not to expect it. She'd chosen it for his sake, not hers, and she'd slowly withered away.

"You're from *Chicago?*"

She sounded so incredulous. He found that amusing.

"It's a big city. You aren't the only person ever born there," he said. "I haven't lived there since I was seven years old and I don't remember much about it. I'd prefer that not to become public knowledge, though." Adriana Gallant would fall all over that piece of gossip.

Elizabeth patted his back. "Your secret is safe with me, Heathcliff."

"Did you call me Heathcliff? As in the emo guy from *Wuthering Heights?*" He wasn't sure how he should take that, although he supposed he'd been called worse.

"I think I'll call you Black Bart from now on," she said.

This ought to be good. "Because…?"

"He was a gentleman bandit with a questionable past who supposedly disappeared into the wilds of Montana after his release from San Quentin."

Sure. That sounded like him. He was impressed that she knew who Black Bart was, though. "You really studied up for this job, didn't you?"

"I really did," she said smugly.

"Then you know Bart was also afraid of horses. I'm not. I've got the Tennessee Walkers to prove it."

"But you prefer horsepower to horses," she said. "Your garage is far more impressive than your stable."

He couldn't argue with that. And the tag Black Bart was better than Heathcliff. "Try calling me Ryan," he advised her, disengaging himself from her arms. She'd relaxed her death grip on him while they talked and it was time to move on from him and his sordid past. "Gather your things. I'll get Steve or Young John to take care of the orphans for you so you can sleep in."

She wasn't finished with her interrogation. "Why did you come back?"

The way she tilted her head when she posed the question made him feel as if his brain were exposed so that she could see inside his head and already knew the answer—because she was the brightest, prettiest distraction he'd come across in forever, with her cascade of curls, amber eyes, and bright mind, and he wanted her.

He'd been standing off to one side of the path, avoiding

the light, watching the bunkhouse from a safe distance, and debating whether or not he should return and take her up on the challenge she'd thrown down.

Because I wanted you to.

"I saw a shadow move where there shouldn't be one," he said.

Then he'd spotted Jonas on the veranda, trapped by the porch light when she opened the door. He'd waited just long enough to see how she'd handle herself. Poorly, as it turned out. She'd given Jonas the benefit of the doubt and he'd seized on it as a weakness. As a result, he'd gotten too close.

That wouldn't happen to her again. She'd become far too important.

He touched her cheek. She caught his hand in hers and turned her lips into his palm, searing a kiss into his flesh. Heat-licked amber eyes, wide and steady, lifted to his.

"We shouldn't do this," she said.

Another challenge thrown down as far as he was concerned. She never learned. "What, exactly, do you think 'this' is?"

"Sex."

Her directness was a never-ending source of entertainment. "And why do you think it would be wrong?"

"Because I work for you."

Technically yes, although it never seemed to stop her from arguing with him.

"It's not going to make for a more awkward situation

between us," he said.

"It's already pretty awkward," she conceded.

His fingers trailed down her throat to toy with the line of her collarbone. "Can you look me in the eye and tell me you aren't wondering what sex between us would be like?"

"Oh, I'm wondering." Her lips bent upward. "And I'm sure it would be fantastic, especially right now, and believe me, I'd like nothing more than to find out. But what happens after?"

She was riding a high. He shouldn't encourage her to make a rash decision that was fueled more by adrenaline than physical attraction, regardless of how much she thought she might want him. That sense of having drifted into uncharted territory jolted him again. Normally, what would matter most was how much he wanted her.

"My timing is off," he said.

"Your timing is perfect," she corrected him, leaving him completely bewildered. "But this is a one-off event. To satisfy mutual curiosity. Do you think you can wake up in the morning and pretend nothing happened?"

He had complete confidence in his personal abilities in that regard. "You've just described my whole philosophy toward sex. What about you?"

She stepped closer. He inhaled the feminine, flowery scent of her hair. She rose to her tiptoes and kissed him, her hands on his shoulders for balance. Heat again licked her amber eyes. "You'd be amazed by how quickly I can forget you."

He laughed out loud at that. "Sweetheart, you keep on tossing out those challenges, why don't you? Because trust me, this will be an experience you'll never forget."

"I'm going to take that as a promise. I want another promise from you, too."

"You really know how to go after a man when he's weak," he complained, although honestly, negotiating sex with her was one of the hottest things he'd ever experienced. "Okay, let's have it. What's this going to cost me?"

"I'm not going to question why you equate sex with money, since it fits in with your philosophy. Which means I'd better get two more promises from you—first, you wear protection."

"Done." He patted his back pocket, which contained his wallet and two foil-wrapped, latex-filled packets. *Thank you, Doctor Dallas, for insisting we always carry condoms on us.* "And the second?" That one made him a whole lot more nervous.

"That you don't use anything about this evening as an excuse to terminate my employment."

Damn it. He didn't care what anyone said. Women definitely knew how—and when—to negotiate, and approached sex far more opportunistically than men. "You think I'd do something like that?"

"Absolutely. I think you'd do it in a heartbeat."

He nipped at her lower lip, then licked it as if it were

candy. She tasted like a sugar high and he couldn't wait to sample every sweet inch of her. It was amazing how quickly he'd gotten over any reluctance to touch her.

"Fine. I promise. This had better be sex I'll never forget either, though," he warned her.

Her palms smoothed the front of his jersey, then edged impatiently into the sleeves of his jacket to nudge it off of his shoulders. "I'll do my best. I'm not sure how I'll stack up against the professionals, though."

"I'm sure you'll score at least a five out of ten. You've got them beat for sarcasm already."

"Speaking of professionals… When was your last check-up?"

"Right before we inherited the ranch. And well after the last time I had sex, so I'm good to go."

"Me too."

He shucked the jacket and tossed it onto one of the empty bunks. It was late. They might as well spend the night here. They could move her things to the house just as easily tomorrow. It crossed his mind that he had a much better bed in his spare room than one of these narrow bunks, but they didn't need a whole lot of room for what he had in mind.

The top three buttons of her blouse were already undone. He reached for the fourth, his attention engaged by the flushed skin underneath. All of his impatience—the anger and fear—had morphed into pure lust, and thoughts about how good she'd feel naked with him deep inside her shoved aside any lingering concerns as to what the morning might bring. He was hard and they were both fully dressed.

Elizabeth, however, hadn't fully bought in. The light clasp of her hands on his wrists brought his traveling fingers to a halt.

"One more thing," she said.

Chapter Nine

Elizabeth

H E HADN'T COME completely down off whatever ledge he'd been walking and she wanted him fully engaged with her, here in the present. He liked to be in control. Therefore, she wanted to see how much he'd willingly relinquish.

"We go at my pace," she said.

His hands fell to his sides. Caution nudged aside the desire in his eyes. "You sure you're okay?"

The question disarmed her. He meant because of the altercation with Jonas. There was so much potential in him for decency and kindness.

"I'm fine." When she reviewed the boy's behavior and tried to make sense out of it, she began to develop some new ideas as to the true source of his aggression. The comment about Angel's dare had tweaked it.

She'd have to puzzle that out later. Ryan was of far more interest to her at the moment. "But you're a control freak, Black Bart. Let's see how far your control will stretch before it snaps."

"Well, isn't that the pot calling the control freak Black Bart," Ryan drawled. He extracted a condom from the wallet in his back pocket and tossed the condom onto the bed. The shiny foil packet sparkled with promise. Desire slid back into his gaze. "But I'm game. What are you into? Whips? Handcuffs? Because I can come up with both."

If she wanted to torture him, she had far better methods. "As intriguing as that sounds, I'm not sure how the labor laws in Montana would hold up against me restraining and whipping my boss. Think of this as another teambuilding exercise. Why don't we see how long you can take orders from me?"

"This should be good. Order away."

"Turn off the light."

"Why?" he asked. "I like to see what I'm doing. Or what's being done to me."

"Aren't we off to a great start?" she said sweetly. "Because I'd rather the entire ranch not see it, too. That's why." The blinds that covered the front window overlooking the path were wide open and she wanted to leave them that way. The moon offered enough light to make things intriguing. "Let's make this a tactile experience. And that's the last explanation I'm giving, by the way."

"Your teambuilding skills could use some finesse." But he reached for the light, plunging the room into darkness.

"That's better. Now lift up your arms and stand still. I

want to take off your clothes."

He did as he was told. Arms raised, he turned to stone.

Her heart pattered like raindrops against the inner walls of her chest as she raised the hem of his shirt. She'd never played sex games with a man before and this might not be the best one to start with. They'd find out soon enough.

With his shirt hiked up to bare his stomach, she bent forward and licked the line between the top of his jeans and his navel. The muscles under his skin tightened, but other than that, and a slight intake of breath, he didn't move. Her hands, holding his shirt out of the way, smoothed over his pecs. She let the shirt drape over her wrists so she could toy with his nipples. They hardened between her thumbs and her fingers. Physically, the man was a serious work of art.

She took one nipple between her lips and caressed it with her tongue. Mounting excitement left her damp and light-headed. He tasted delicious.

And to think, she could taste and touch him for the rest of the night, if she chose.

"Take off your shirt," she said. She wasn't tall enough to remove it herself.

The fabric rustled, then fell to the floor a few feet away. Fortunately, he wasn't wearing boots. She knelt and removed one shoe, then the other, along with his socks. He had beautiful feet, too. Long and slender. She ran her hand the length of one sole, making his toes curl. She pressed a kiss to his ankle, rose, and reached for the button at the fly of his jeans. Here would be the real test of his control.

She took a few steps back. There was enough light in the room for her to see the way he watched her—the way a cat feigned disinterest until its prey wandered too close. She kicked her shoes off, and slowly, one by one, unbuttoned her shirt. She let it fall from her shoulders, then reached behind her and unfastened her bra. It followed her shirt. Cool air rippled over her breasts. Now they were both wearing only their jeans.

"Tell me what you're thinking," she said.

"I'm thinking," he replied, sounding far too conversational for her peace of mind, "that the next time we play this game I'll have you undressed a lot faster than this, but that's where things will slow down. Within two minutes you'll be begging me for satisfaction, and I'll give it to you, but not until I'm good and ready."

"Someone's ego is healthy. But this was for one night, remember?"

"We agreed to pretend it never happened. No one said anything about one night."

The pattering in her chest increased to a downpour. This was what she got for striking deals with the devil. She'd debate that with him later. Right now, her common sense was engaged elsewhere.

She wriggled out of her jeans, watching him watch her. Now she wore nothing but a scrap of lace.

His gaze zeroed in on it. She heard him swallow. "Dear

God. That's what case managers consider panties?"

"I can't speak for everyone. But it's what I choose to wear."

"You're determined to make tomorrow morning as hard for me as possible, aren't you?" he sighed.

"I'm trying to make you hard tonight," she replied. She ran a daring palm over the large bulge in his jeans and offered him a sweet smile of satisfaction. "Mission accomplished."

He growled low in his throat. "Move it along, Elizabeth. You don't want to know what's going to happen to you if my control really does snap."

"You've made it this far. I'll take my chances." She eased his zipper down, carefully, and slid her hand into his jeans. The impressive bulge sprang free of his boxers.

She wasn't a stranger to male anatomy, despite her father's best efforts. She'd had several lovers, although none serious enough to take home to meet her parents. But Ryan, she conceded, brought a whole new level of competition to the game.

She eased his jeans and shorts over his hips, drifting to her knees as she lowered the last of his clothes to the floor. She freed first one foot, then the other, and pushed the garments out of the way. She considered the erect penis standing at attention a few inches above her head. She planned to taste it, too. And as much of him as she could.

But not yet.

She licked the inside of a thigh, well-toned from ranch labor, then got to her feet. She gave the velvety soft head of his penis a brush of her lips as a promise on her way past.

"Take off my panties," she said.

He slid his hands over the cheeks of her buttocks and down the backs of her legs while he was at it. Since she'd fully expected him to take advantage, and anticipated it with a large degree of excitement, the sensations caused by the rough texture of his work-hardened hands were exquisite. When he'd said he could have her begging for him within two minutes, he hadn't been kidding.

He needed to be reminded of who was in control. She took hold of one of his hands. "Touch me. Here." She guided it between her legs.

"You're playing with fire," he warned her, his jaw muscles flexing.

"I hear a lot of talk. Let's see some action." Her words exploded on short clips of breath dripping with need. His losing control didn't seem like a bad thing, anymore. She was all for it, in fact.

He slid one finger inside her, and began to ease it in and out, stroking her until she could focus on nothing except the pleasure he gave. She wriggled her hips, rubbing against the heel of his palm while encouraging his action. She'd wanted this. She'd wanted *him*. She hadn't realized how much. A quivering began, deep in her lower belly, and she gasped. She was seconds from coming.

He knew it.

"That does it. Game's over," he said, and hoisted her into his arms. She wrapped her arms around his neck and her legs around his waist. His mouth nuzzled her throat as he strode to the bed.

"Not yet," she said, now that she'd had a few seconds of sanity. She eased her hand between their two bodies and cupped the hot, heavy weight of him in her palm. She gently squeezed his shaft, flicking the blunt of her thumb over the damp tip.

He made a sound deep in his throat and flipped her onto her back on the bed. He grabbed for the condom. "Yes, yet."

She scrambled to her knees and reached for him again. "One more minute."

"You've got thirty seconds. I'm counting."

She kissed the tip of his penis. She'd never get it all in her mouth, so she concentrated on the head, tracing her tongue around the rim. He dug his fingers into her hair, cradling her head. She clasped the backs of his thighs, feeling their strength as he trembled to keep from thrusting.

Impressive.

She fell back on the bed, tossing her arms above her head on the pillow. She grabbed onto the headboard and parted her knees. "Make me beg," she commanded. His eyes glittered in the thin moonlight as they ran the length of her naked and exposed inner thighs. She arched her hips. "Any time now."

He planted one knee on the bed and swung the other across her body. He captured her hands in one of his and leaned on one arm, staring down at her for long seconds. His thick penis throbbed against her belly, demanding attention she longed to give it, but he had her hands pinned.

"God, you're beautiful," he said, running a thumb across her cheek with a gentle, restrained tenderness that shocked her, considering the source.

He sat upright, his weight on his knees, and taking his shaft in his hand, ripped open the packet with his teeth before rolling the condom into place. He positioned himself between her thighs and guided the head of his erection inside her—but only the head. He slowly withdrew, his eyes on her face. Eased in. Withdrew again. By now, Elizabeth was writhing beneath him. He again had her on the brink of an orgasm, and yet seemed in no hurry to satisfy it.

She heard herself begging. She arched her back, trying to take him fully inside her. "Please, Ryan. Now. I'm going to come."

"Not yet," he said.

"*Yes*, yet. You can't control when I orgasm." The nerve of the man.

He ran a roughened hand from the swell of her breast to the curve of her hip. "I most definitely can," he assured her, arrogantly confident. "And you're going to come twice."

He kept her hands pinned above her. Then, when she didn't think she could take another second of torture, a hard, single thrust had him firmly where he belonged.

"Oh, my God," she cried out, shaking with pleasure.

Ryan was far from finished illustrating exactly how much control he had over her. He waited for the tiny spasms of her inner muscles to subside, then began a slow, deliberate attempt to restimulate them—with resounding success. He drew the tip of one breast into his mouth, then the other. The harsh, guttural sounds he made as his movements quickened and deepened soon had her on the edge of a second orgasm she hadn't known was a possibility. His hips tightened. His fingers clenched around her hands. He dropped his chin. Another thrust, a muttered expletive, and he came—at the same moment she did.

He remained inside her, both of them too tired and satisfied to move, although he was careful not to let his full weight fall on her, but carried it in his forearms pressed to either side of her head. The bed was too narrow for them to lie side by side. He kissed her, as slowly and deeply and thoroughly as he'd made love to her. If he continued to kiss her that way, a third orgasm was definitely on the table.

She had no idea what was happening between them. She did know that never again was she going to tease him about his level of control. He'd proved himself. Splendidly.

Except for one crucial detail.

"Oh, my God," Elizabeth said, repeating herself, but for an entirely new and unwelcome reason.

Ryan

"THE WORDS ARE right, but the tone seems off. What's wrong?"

Because Ryan couldn't imagine. The sex had been as amazing as he'd known it would be, to the point he'd begun to ponder various ways in which he could make her beg for it twice in one night. Since she'd been as engaged as he was, the chances she was experiencing regret seemed remote—although not off the table.

She pushed at his chest. "Condoms can leak."

The horror of that possibility had him forgetting about another round of sex and withdrawing in haste. Unfortunately, the condom didn't feel the same sense of urgency.

He swore.

"What?" Elizabeth demanded, digging her elbows into the mattress and struggling to sit up.

He braced his forearm across her chest to keep her from wriggling around. "Hold still. We've got a slight problem."

She'd figured out what had gone wrong. A hint of hysteria crept into her voice. "Do you *think*?"

He reached down and retrieved the spent condom, and pinching it closed, held it aloft. Relief and panic duked it out while he weighed the odds for disaster, but he tag-teamed logic into their battle so Elizabeth wouldn't freak out alongside him. "False alarm. I've got it."

He carried the condom into the bathroom and disposed of it. When he returned, he settled into the single bed so that she was half on top of him. He pressed her head to his chest and combed his fingers through her tangled curls, working through the knots. "Depending on where you are in your cycle, there's only about a twenty percent chance of you getting pregnant."

"I know the odds. I'm a social worker. That's not the point. We should both know better than this. We're not teenagers." She jabbed him with a finger. "And the proper expression is 'us getting pregnant,' not 'you.'"

"Fair enough. I don't want a pregnancy any more than you do, regardless of how we choose to phrase it. But let's not borrow trouble over something that's not likely to happen," he said. Since she was a social worker, she knew what their options were. If the worst did occur, he'd tell her what the zygote's makeup consisted of and they'd deal with it then. That was one DNA string he planned to get snipped as soon as he could, and the current situation merely confirmed the necessity, because bringing another Cienetti into the world was not going to happen. "Are you in the danger zone or not?"

He could almost hear the wheels in her head spinning as she calculated the days. "Not. But I'm going to pick up the morning-after pill as soon as the pharmacy opens on Monday, just to be safe. I've got seventy-two hours."

Thank God, they were on the same page.

"Then," he said, taking her hand and placing it firmly on his growing expression of interest, and helping her slide her fingers up and down as a less than subtle reminder of how much fun they'd been having, "there's no sense in stressing about it. Why don't we get back to more important matters?"

It didn't take much convincing. Elizabeth was as forthright about sex and what pleased her as she was about everything else. If anything, she was downright bossy in bed. He'd never been especially good at taking orders, but for her, he'd make an exception.

Much later, long after she dropped off to sleep, he lay awake in the dark and played with a lock of her hair, twining it around his finger.

He had no intentions of leaving her alone yet, although he planned to be gone before sunrise. He didn't give a damn who knew they were sleeping together, but since it wasn't his professional reputation at risk, that wasn't his call to make. She had to work with the Grand school system's superintendent and the local school board, none of whom were known for their liberal ideas. She was an Easterner—that was already one strike against her. He'd come back right after breakfast and help her pack up.

His more immediate concern was what the sleeping arrangements would be after she moved to the house. The sex was shaping up to be off the charts—just thinking about the soft little panting moans that erupted from her when she came was an instant hard-on revitalizer—but she was right about them keeping their relationship outside of working hours strictly to that.

Eventually, once more women were hired, she'd have to move back into the bunkhouse, so having her stay in the guest suite as planned would be best, and overall, less—messy, was the best word he could find to describe it. It didn't mean he couldn't spend the occasional night in the guest suite while she was there, too.

He hadn't forgotten about that little shit, Jonas. Now that he had Elizabeth safe in his arms, and for the foreseeable future, he could think somewhat more coherently about what had happened. The punishment stood. Jonas would be pounding fence posts for the next month. Ryan planned to have a talk with his counselor and Handy right after breakfast and make the arrangements.

He dozed off for a bit, but as soon as light began to filter into the bunkhouse, casting streams of gold across the plain hardwood floor, he eased out from under Elizabeth's limp weight, got dressed, and walked the path to the house. A quick phone call ensured one of the hands would take care of the newborns for her so she could sleep.

He let himself into the main house just as Dan was exiting his suite. He wore his sheriff's uniform, which wasn't a good sign before sunup on a Sunday morning.

"You're getting home late," Dan said, jiggling the keys in

his hand.

"No—I'm getting up right on schedule," Ryan replied. "This is a working ranch. Someone has to run it."

Dan gave him a long look. "If you were on schedule, you'd be heading out the door, not in. You'd be wearing boots and a coverall, too. And your shirt wouldn't be inside out."

"Don't you have somewhere important to be?" Ryan asked.

"Not especially. I'm taking the tail end of a shift for one of the deputies because his wife went into labor. Maybe I should ask you the same question. Don't you have somewhere important to be?" Dan grinned. "Or maybe somewhere important you've been?"

"You're an ass. You know that—right?"

"Just glad you're finally getting some." Dan's grin widened. "You were starting to make Dallie and me twitchy, too. Now we don't have to feel as sorry for you."

"Nice. And yet oddly, I still feel sorry for Jazz and Hannah. You're mistaken, however." He filled Dan in on what had happened with Jonas and what the punishment would be. "I warned you about this, didn't I?"

"You did," Dan conceded. His dark blond brows pinched together. "But the responsibility for it's on us. He shouldn't have been able to get out of his bunk after hours without the counselor knowing about it. What was the level of intent?"

"Level of intent?" Ryan echoed.

"First, he left her a note. The note in itself was harmless enough. Juvenile, really. Why was he on her doorstep after the movie last night, though? What was his reason for seeking her out? What harm did he intend her, if any?" He held up a hand when he read Ryan's expression. "I'm basing my questions on the law, in case this goes any further and we have to lawyer up, because believe me, that's the first thing his family will do. Elizabeth might too, so bear with me. Did he touch her in any way? If so, did he commit a misdemeanor or a felony?"

Ryan hated it when Dan went all law-abiding and neutral. "He didn't touch her." That was why he was alive. A commitment to non-violence only stretched to a point. "He was leaving flowers on her doorstep."

"And how do you know this?"

"I saw it."

"From inside or outside the bunkhouse?"

"Jesus, Dan. Am I on trial?"

"I want you to put this in the proper perspective. You can get too one-sided when you believe someone you care about or feel responsible for has a problem."

Ryan would like to argue, but the facts were against him. He'd once offered to buy off Jazz's dodgy family to keep them away from Dan and his money. "From outside, okay? It was late. I walked her home."

"You walked her home to a bunkhouse within sight of

the house and the other bunkhouses on the ranch. That might suggest you were aware there was a danger."

"It's a ranch. The danger could be from bears, especially when we've got calves in the pens."

"True." Dan paused as if gathering more ammunition and loading his gun, then continued. "After you left her, you saw Jonas leave flowers on her doorstep. What did you do?"

"Nothing."

"Nothing?" Dan blinked. "That's so unlike you."

"I didn't get a chance to do anything. Elizabeth opened the door, so I waited to see what happened next."

"You waited." Dan rubbed his forehead with his thumb. "That will look good on the Endeavour in court... Okay. It was late. The kid was there to leave flowers. Why would she open the door?"

That right there was the one door Ryan had no intentions of opening when Dan was in inquisition mode like this. She'd opened it because she'd thought it was him, calling her bluff. "How should I know?"

"Did he knock?"

"No."

"What happened after she opened the door?"

"I was too far away to hear what was said, but she was all pokered up with her social worker face on. She said something I couldn't hear, but she didn't look pleased. She took the flowers from him. That was when I moved in. By the time I got there, he was trying to muscle into the bunkhouse on the pretext of wanting a glass of water."

"Mistake, letting him get that close," Dan said with a wince, shifting from impartial lawman to someone who'd responded to more than one call related to violence against women. "You say he tried to muscle his way in. Did he physically touch her or did he verbally threaten her?"

"Neither. But she was intimidated."

"Because she felt threatened by him personally, or because by the nature of her work, she's too well-informed with regard to its risks? Or was she intimidated by a teenaged boy because of her sister?"

"Too far, Dan," Ryan said.

"She opened the door, buddy. Physically as well as metaphorically. Those are exactly the kinds of questions you need to be asking yourself before you take that kid's head off or have Handy work him to death. Or, for that matter, while filling out the incident report. Don't forget that needs to be done." Dan clapped him on the shoulder. "Still doesn't explain why your shirt's inside out, though."

"Go hand out parking tickets," Ryan said sourly.

Dan, however, had given him plenty to ponder.

It was true that he hadn't heard their whole conversation, and his perspective on what he'd seen might be somewhat colored by his past history with violence and need for control, especially since Elizabeth had far too much confidence in her abilities to take care of herself. No way could she break someone's leg.

Therefore, that was his job.

Metaphorically speaking.

A quick check of the clock said he had roughly one more hour before heading back to the bunkhouse to help her move her belongings. He had one thing to take care of first.

He called Handy and invited him up to the office where they could talk in private. He explained to him how Jonas had been caught leaving his bunk after hours and that he'd be pounding fence posts and stringing wire with Handy for the next month as punishment.

"How come I'm the one being punished?" Handy complained. "I didn't sign on to babysit spoiled little rich kids."

And Ryan had never intended to be in a position where he'd be protecting women from them. Everyone had their problems.

"I hear the Running River Ranch is hiring," he said mildly.

"Work for Weldon Scott?" Handy made a face as if he'd smelled something rotten. "Forget that idea. The spoiled little rich kid is about to learn what it's like to work for a living."

Chapter Ten

Elizabeth

E LIZABETH WOKE UP alone, which didn't surprise her. Heathcliff had issues with intimacy completely separate from sex.

My dad wasn't one of the good guys.

In Chicago-speak, she knew what that likely meant. His mother fleeing the state with him, and his lack of a past, were two more good clues. Thanks to her studies and advocacy work, she'd heard quite a few true stories with similar themes of targeted hits, but she didn't know of any Chicago O'Connells who might fit Ryan's story.

Everything, combined with the money he'd inherited from an unknown benefactor, left her thinking she should leave well enough alone and not dig too deep. At the end of the day, his past remained none of her business and she planned to keep it that way. They'd had one night of sex when emotions ran high.

While she wouldn't call it a mistake, despite the unfortunate condom mishap—she'd take care of that first thing tomorrow—she'd been smart to get his agreement before-hand that this was a one-off event and he couldn't use it against her. He seized on weakness the way a lion went after the lame. He liked to play with his kill too.

Her phone, buried somewhere beneath carelessly discard-ed clothing, pinged an alert that she'd gotten a text.

She stretched, stark naked—not her usual state when she woke up in the morning—and rolled from the bunk. Cold floorboards kissed the soles of her feet. She snatched up her robe and slippers from the shower next to the kitchen before rushing to draw the blinds she hadn't wanted to close during the previous night's teambuilding exercises.

The text was from Ryan, letting her know he'd be there in an hour to begin moving her belongings. She frowned at it.

Now that daylight had arrived, the incident with Jonas became far less sinister. That, and the sunlight doing its best to warm up the floor, had her rethinking her hasty agree-ment to move. Yes, Jonas had been too aggressive by far, but when she considered the nuances of his behavior, she saw what had bothered her—there'd been nothing sexual about it.

A mental review of his profile, where he'd initially exhib-ited violence over not making a male-dominated sports team, and a check of her research notes on him, suggested possible confusion over his sexual orientation might be the real culprit. He claimed to have acted on a dare from Angel, who was an extraordinarily good-looking, dominant, and promiscuous boy—exactly the type Jonas would want to impress. Her fleeing in fear to the main house wasn't going to send him the right message at all.

Unfortunately, she'd agreed to the move, so the damage was done. If she tried to change her mind now, Heathcliff would lose his. She'd give it a few days and then ask him if they could review other options.

An hour later, when he arrived, she had her bags packed and ready to go. She waited to see how he'd behave after promising he'd forget all about the night before. If she'd thought he'd be possessive, or in any way romantic, she had no reason to worry.

He grabbed her belongings and hoisted them onto a small utility vehicle, called a Gator, that to her looked more like a golf cart than a piece of farm equipment. She latched the bunkhouse door on mixed feelings and hopped into the passenger seat of the Gator.

Ryan's guest suite hadn't changed since she'd stayed in it the night of the blizzard. She had a small sitting room with a desk and bookshelves in it so she could work on her dissertation, a bedroom with a queen-sized bed, and an enormous bathtub in the en suite that made the move well worth her while.

Rather than leave her to unpack alone, Ryan sprawled on the bed. He folded his arms behind his head and crossed his long legs at the ankles and proceeded to watch her.

She crammed a handful of panties into a drawer, opting to tidy them later. "Don't you have any hobbies?"

"One. It takes teamwork."

She grabbed another suitcase and unzipped it, determined to ignore him.

"Good God," he said. "How many pairs of shoes do you own?"

She re-zipped the suitcase and pushed it aside, then sat on her heels on the floor, her hands on her thighs. They had to talk and there was no time like the present.

"About last night," she began.

"You're welcome."

The way his eyes lingered on her threatened to derail her. Only dogged determination kept her on track. "I meant after Jonas left."

"So did I."

His smugness wasn't entirely undeserved. Despite knowing better than to sleep with her boss, that was what she'd done. She'd exhibited weakness. "Maybe we should revisit the ground rules for our new living arrangements. I thought we were going to pretend last night never happened."

"I am pretending last night never happened," he said. "Since we're now living together, I'm a whole lot more interested in what happens tonight."

She knew he enjoyed provoking her, and the proper response in this situation was to ignore the provocation, but she couldn't seem to use her common sense around him.

Last night was an excellent example. "We're not living together."

"Tell that to the church and the state of Montana."

The next smartest move would be to distance herself from the source of the provocation. "There's no point in talking to you if you aren't going to be serious."

She went to the sitting room to unpack her books and her laptop, more annoyed with herself than his teasing, because she liked it too much when he switched from Heathcliff to Black Bart. She liked him too much, period, considering survivors of violent crime, like Ryan, often developed severe anger issues. He'd translated his into a powerful need for control. In that respect, he was much like her father.

That last observation brought her unpacking to a halt. She dropped the stack of books she'd removed from a box on the desk. It turned out Ryan wasn't the only one who had issues left over from violent crime—which wasn't disturbing at all. She might want to give the reason behind her attraction to him more serious consideration.

She finished with her books and moved on to the next bag of her belongings. When she returned to the bedroom to put a stack of clothes in the closet, she discovered he'd fallen asleep.

Sleep didn't soften him as much as one might expect. From the navy plaid work shirt worn over a matching T-shirt, to the wash-faded jeans with stains ground into the fibers, and hand-knit wool socks—she wondered where those had come from—he looked every inch the work-hardened rancher. He had one arm thrown over his eyes and a slight frown on his lips—more thoughtful than morose, as if even his dreams were problems in need of a solution.

And he was a problem solver, no doubt about it. If the bits and pieces of conversations she'd overheard coming from his office were true indicators, it was amazing what he'd managed to accomplish with the ranch in just over a year.

She shoved the pile of clothes haphazardly onto a shelf and tiptoed to the side of the bed. A man like this would have thrived in pioneer days, back when Montana was settled. He would have bent the land to his will—it would never have bent him.

Desire stroked up the insides of her thighs to her belly. She'd assumed the previous night had been ignited by circumstances—first the moonlit walk, the sweet talk and the kiss, then his ride to her rescue. Not so. She'd wanted him long before that.

He was so unlike any man she'd known in Chicago. She didn't know what to do. She'd never found herself in a situation like this, where her personal and professional lives intersected with such intense and conflicting results.

She touched his leg. He didn't stir. She tracked her finger up his thigh, over his hip, to his stomach. No reaction. She splayed her widened palm on his chest, curious as to how deeply he slept.

Strong fingers closed over her wrist and jerked her forward. She tumbled onto the bed with a cry of surprise on her lips and a thin smile on his. He'd raised his head from the pillows. Sleep-licked eyes gazed steadily into hers. Light from the window caught the bright blue ringing the outer edges of his brown pupils.

"Really, Elizabeth," he said. "Is this how you plan to pretend nothing happened?"

"I..." She could think of nothing to say. This was her second show of weakness.

He rolled toward her, pinning her free arm between them, and stretched her imprisoned hand over her head, so that both arms were trapped. He kissed the sensitive underside of her jaw.

"How about if we save pretending nothing happened for later?" he suggested, the words whisper soft in her ear. He followed up with another light kiss, this one to the base of her throat. Warm breath feathered her skin, and sexual awareness, drunken and wild, reignited. She lost any urge to object to the hand inching under her sweater, instead welcoming the exploring touch of her body as her answer.

Seconds later, he'd discarded her sweater and bra. His hands cupped her breasts while she worked on the fly of his jeans. She had him in her palm and was stroking his velvet-skinned hardness when she remembered what was missing.

"We don't have any condoms," she said.

He tipped her onto her back on the bed and tugged off

her trousers and panties. He shed his clothes, reached for the drawer in the small bedside table, and withdrew a foil packet. "We have three dozen, ultra-thin, ribbed condoms right here. That should last us for the next day or so." He knelt astride her on the bed, his knees on either side of her hips, and held up the packet. He wore a drowsy, very sensual, decidedly non-Heathcliff smile. "Would you like to do the honors, or shall I?"

She was too distracted by how lovely he looked naked to hear what he said. His leanness was deceptive. Long, corded calves supported thighs thick with muscle. He had the elegant grace of a gymnast. The moves to match, too. Hot male sexuality dripped from every tongue-licking line of his body. He sucked in a breath as she ran one fingertip from the flat plane of his belly to the underside of his erection.

"You keep doing what you're doing," he said, dark eyes amused. Ruffled brown hair fell over his brow. "I'll take care of the rest." He moved to tear open the packet.

Elizabeth caught his hand. If their relationship outside of work was to be purely about sex, they had control issues—trust ones, too—that they'd have to confront. She'd never had any urge to play sex games before, but rattling that rampant male ego of his offered too much temptation. "How do you feel about bondage?"

He froze, as if sensing a sudden shift in the wind. "You or me?"

"Me." Since she'd suggested this, she should go first.

Plus, on the surface, it appeared to place him in control and her in a position of trust, the opposite of last night. She poked his male ego a little. "I never pictured you as a strictly missionary kind of guy. Is it a problem?"

He didn't precisely relax, but he no longer appeared quite so tightly wound. "Just surprised. Got any scarves?"

She scrambled from the bed and dug through one of her bags. She came up with three and held them out for his inspection. "We could use a T-shirt for the fourth," she suggested.

His eyes said he wanted to laugh, but his expression remained serious. "It's a bed, not a torture rack. Two will be plenty."

She saw what he meant. She was short, so there was no way she could be tied to all four of the bedposts unless they had something much longer. She passed him the scarves and he tied her hands over her head. He left the knots loose.

"What about a safe word?" She should have asked that particular question before her wrists were secured, not after.

"I'll never do anything to you that a simple 'stop' won't be sufficient." His eyes glittered with promise. "My immediate goal is to make you say, 'Don't stop.'"

"I like your confidence. My expectations are now really high, Black Bart."

"Have no fear. A gentleman never leaves a lady disappointed. And those of us who aren't exactly gentlemen tend to be overachievers." He parted her thighs with his hands and held them wide with his knees. "You sure you're okay with this?"

"I'm fine. Can we move things along? I can't ask you not to stop if you never get started," she said.

"Unbelievable… Who's in charge here—you or me?"

He placed a kiss on her belly. His thumbs stroked her skin as he held her hips steady.

Then, sitting back on his heels, he again reached for the condom. He leisurely rolled it over his erection, taking his time while she watched. It seemed he had a bit of exhibitionism to go along with all that self-confidence.

Anticipation tightened her toes. The position of voyeur wasn't such a bad spot to be in, particularly when the object of scrutiny was an incredibly hot cowboy with a side sizzle of dark, Byronic hero thrown in.

He eased the tip of his erection inside her, very slowly, then a little farther, until they were fully joined. He began to withdraw, maintaining the same slow, steady pace, keeping his eyes on her face. A light line of sweat appeared at the hairline of his forehead, but other than that, he appeared unperturbed by his less than sufficient performance, acting as if he hadn't a care in the world. In reality, if he didn't step up his game, he had seconds to live.

Then, he pulled out completely, leaving her without satisfaction and aching with need.

She could have wept. "Are you out of your mind?"

He cupped a hand to his ear. "What was that? Did you

have something you wanted to say?"

"Don't make me have to finish this myself."

Both eyebrows went up. "This, I want to see. How do you plan to do that with your hands tied?"

"You told me this bed wasn't a torture rack."

"You probably should have insisted on that safe word. It turns out I have more of a taste for torture than I thought."

She tried to decide if she loved seeing this side of him or if she planned to kill him once they were done. "You win, Black Bart." She wriggled her hips. "Don't stop. I'm begging you. Please."

"You could sound more sincere."

"You're a dead man. I mean it. How's that for sincere?"

He laughed at her, the sadist. "Good enough."

He took himself in hand and slid into position. She hooked her heels over the backs of his thighs. He didn't get to pull out again. Not before they were both satisfied.

She needn't have worried. He threw himself in with far greater enthusiasm this round. The headboard creaked under the strain of her bound hands struggling for freedom, unused to a lack of participation, which only served to tighten the knots. Bondage—this total dependency on another for pleasure—was more intensely erotic than she'd imagined.

Heat exploded like a rogue ocean wave from the insides of her thighs. The rippling of tightly coiled inner muscles against the hard length of his erection elicited a swear word from him. Her orgasm preceded his by a fraction of a second.

He collapsed next to her, one hand on her breast, his chest heaving. When he got his breath back, he disposed of the used condom and untied her hands. She was too limp to move more than her head as she watched the deft play of his fingers as they worked the knots loose. He dragged the tip of his finger down the line of her nose, then kissed her. She smiled up at him. He was fun in bed.

"Well, that was unexpected," she said.

Ryan

SOMEONE HURLED A rock through Ryan's bedroom window while he was taking a shower.

He rushed out of the bathroom, naked and dripping wet, to find shards of broken glass sprinkled across the cream-colored carpet. He pressed against the wall, away from the glass, and lifted the side of the heavy curtain, peering out in time to see Jonas hurdling a hedge and making a mad dash for the barns.

He let the curtain fall back into place. A logical conclusion would be that someone had either told Jonas how he'd be spending the next month, or the boy objected to Elizabeth moving into the house. Maybe both.

He'd have to reconsider his stance that the Endeavour

wasn't a prison. He didn't care about the cost of the vandal-ism so much as the inconvenience it created.

He tramped back into the bathroom in search of a towel and his clothes and thought through his next move while drying his hair. He considered not telling Elizabeth about the broken window, but quickly discarded the idea. If he didn't, and she found out, it would open the door for her to keep things from him. So far, she hadn't. He'd like to keep things that way. The silver lining was that he'd have an excuse to sleep in her room until he got the carpet cleaned and the window repaired. Not a good one, perhaps. But good enough.

He'd had her three times so far—twice last night and again this morning—and it hadn't taken more than the edge off. He'd even allowed her a game of bondage—something he'd normally never agree to—all because the idea intrigued her. He'd entertained thoughts of her with him while he showered, the water flowing over her pale, lovely skin, her legs wrapped around his hips, and was considering ways to make that fantasy happen.

What he wouldn't think about just yet was how they'd deal with her probationary period when it was up. Their boss-employee relationship was almost as great a complica-tion as Jonas's obsession with her, but they'd traveled too far down that road to reverse course and they might as well enjoy the trip while it lasted. He didn't know where it might end.

He made a few calls and arranged for the broken window to be boarded up with plywood until it could be replaced. When he emerged from his bedroom, Elizabeth was cutting through the living room on her way out.

"Where are you going?" he asked.

"The cookhouse. It's lunchtime."

"Or we can eat here. Together."

"Boundaries, remember?" She exuded patience as she reverted to her professional persona. He settled in to be wowed by her logic. "I think we should carry on business as usual. I missed breakfast, and soon, everyone will be wondering why I moved to the main house. What should I tell them?"

"That we needed the space for Dallas's brothers. The boys are planning to come up next weekend. The oldest is twenty-one and the youngest is nineteen. That's where they usually stay when they're here."

Her lower lip puckered as she flipped his suggestion around, searching for flaws. It never failed to amaze him that she believed he was the one with control issues. Even bound to the headboard, she'd been bossy. The recollection sent his thoughts in a whole different direction.

"No one will think it weird?" she asked, drawing him back.

He didn't care if they did. "Dallas was complaining because it meant he wouldn't have Hannah all to himself. They were complaining because they didn't want to—how did they put it—listen to the horizontal mambo all night long."

"That's sweet. I mean that Dallas wants Hannah to himself," Elizabeth said.

And he wanted Elizabeth all to himself, so she should be more understanding as to why he didn't want her hanging out in the cookhouse with the men anymore. Yes. He had a streak of possessiveness. It wasn't his worst character flaw.

"Dan's mother keeps our kitchens well-stocked for us. There's no reason for you to eat at the cookhouse while you stay here."

Stubbornness came naturally to her. It was one of the many reasons she intrigued him so much. Normally, no one argued with him. The ranch hands certainly didn't. She drew herself up to her full height of five nothing, prepared to explain why she was right and he was wrong until she'd beaten him down. Meanwhile, the curly red ponytail and freshly scrubbed face, along with the soft curves of her breasts under the pearl-buttoned pink sweater, had him thinking lunch was overrated and maybe they should return to bed for the rest of the day.

"Are you listening to me?" she asked.

He dragged his eyes upward to hers, where impatience burned through the amber, sparking off buried flecks of gold. He liked playing this game with her, where she tried to defeat him with logic. She usually won, too—which was why he didn't mind cheating every now and then to keep things somewhat even.

"Yes, I'm listening. You said you expect me to treat you the same as I would every other employee on the ranch, although I hope you mean outside of the bedroom. I'm good with that, and here's how it's going to be. Since I'm in charge, and I expect my employees to do as they're told, from now on, you'll eat your meals here."

If she'd been anyone else, she would have flipped him off, but she was too classy for that. He stayed an arm's length out of reach though, in case she decided more teambuilding was warranted.

"I'll be working on my dissertation after lunch," she said, giving up with an ease that left him suspicious, then turned her back on him and walked out of the room—headed, no doubt, for the outdoors and the cookhouse, in direct violation of his orders and how she claimed she wished to be treated.

That was okay. The pint-sized pixie was an endless source of entertainment. He hadn't expected anything different from her, since she'd already made up her mind. He could eat in the cookhouse too, if that was how she wanted to play this. She wasn't the only one who knew how to get their own way.

He gave her a head start. When he arrived at the cookhouse, she'd joined Ace, Jonas, and Tyce at their table and was carrying on a conversation with them as if last night never happened.

Considerably less entertained now than before, he

grabbed a tray, loaded it with a bowl of chili and biscuits, then set his tray next to hers on the table, forcing Tyce to make room. He dragged a chair over, sat down, and grinned across the table at Jonas, who ducked his head over his food to avoid making eye contact.

"How are we all doing?" Ryan asked, looking around to include everyone present before singling him out. "Jonas. I hear you're helping out with the fencing all summer." *That's right, pal. That broken window bought you the whole summer.*

He'd forgotten to tell Elizabeth about it, though. He'd have to remember to do that later.

"Handy says I'll build muscle," Jonas replied, accepting the news as if it were some sort of privilege, which would have pissed Ryan off a lot more, except he'd been a jerk as a teen, too.

Still could be. "Bet he didn't mention the blackflies." Elizabeth kicked his ankle under the table. He rested his elbow on the back of her chair in retaliation. The tip of her ponytail tickled his sleeve, providing a bright splash of color against the drab gray of the fabric. "You'll see plenty of wildlife, too. Better stick close to Handy. He'll have the bear spray and the rifle." Because it wasn't as if anyone would let the kid carry a weapon.

"This is why you should stay in your bunks after lights out," Ace said to the boys. "If you don't, we feed you to the bears."

"You aren't funny." Elizabeth seared both men with her

case manager glare, a reminder they were supposed to be the adults in the room.

"We weren't trying to be funny. I'm serious," Ryan replied. "Stay close to Handy," he said to Jonas. The kid was too cocky by far. He'd like him to learn a lesson or two, but he didn't intend for any harm to come to him while he did. "Cattle attract bears because they make an easy meal, especially the calves, but at the end of the day, bears aren't too fussy about what they eat."

Elizabeth picked up her tray, her lunch barely half finished. "There goes my appetite. Have a nice afternoon, gentlemen."

Ryan reviewed what he'd said. Bears might not have been the right topic to bring up in front of a city girl who was already wary of night noises on a ranch. She was pretty attached to the bottle-fed orphans, too. She'd be thinking of them out there without any mother to protect them.

And oddly enough, even after last night, she genuinely cared what happened to Jonas. He did too, when it came right down to it. But the little dumbass was here to learn lessons, and the lessons were about to begin.

Owen, who'd been following the conversation with unabashed interest, leaned over from his table beside them. "Maybe next Saturday night, you should be the one to pick out a movie that will impress girls," he suggested to Ryan. "You sound like an expert."

Chapter Eleven

Elizabeth

A KNOCK ON the door to the guest suite interrupted Elizabeth's review of her handwritten notes. Since it could only be one person, the guesswork wasn't taxing.

She set the notebook aside.

She'd done her research on bear attacks before she came to Montana and she knew the statistics. The bear population here in the south-central part of the state wasn't as large as that of the western mountainous regions around Missoula, either. She also knew that grizzlies were protected under the Endangered Species Act and avoiding them altogether was preferable to shooting one and then having to prove it was self-defense after. Black bears were more common, and the chance they'd attack a human much more remote—but not an impossibility.

However, stalking off from lunch like a child hadn't been her most professional move and served to highlight that she had her own emotional issues. While logically, she understood her fear of Montana wildlife stemmed from a fear of the unknown—when she'd been eleven no one had discussed Marianne's murder with her, so she'd been left to her own imagination—it didn't make it any less real. The two personalities of this new Dr. Jekyll and Mr. Hyde relationship with Ryan added another layer of confusion to her position at the ranch for her to sort out.

The door opened a crack.

"Mind if I come in?" Ryan asked.

"It's your house."

"This is your space. I won't intrude if you don't want me to."

The happy fluttering in her chest was ridiculous, and all because he'd made a concession she hadn't expected. She scooted over to create room for him on the settee. "I want you to."

She assumed he'd begin with an apology for baiting Jonas, but it turned out she was wrong about that too.

"He threw a rock through your window?" That was an increasingly bold turn of events. "Are you sure it was him?" she asked, trying to imagine the nerve it would take. Ryan didn't exactly come across as warm and understanding. He definitely wasn't the type to overlook a transgression.

"Positive. I saw him."

Which explained why Jonas had been sentenced to work in the fields for the entire summer and not the original month. It didn't justify Ryan putting a troubled boy with no ranching experience in a dangerous situation.

"He's not in any danger," Ryan assured her when she voiced her concern. "Handy will take care of him. It's not as if bears are scouring the range, looking for idiot teenagers to eat. They have other—some might argue better—menu options."

"You still aren't funny."

"I'm still not trying to be. Cattle are more of a threat to the men when they're fencing. Some of them get pretty wild, especially the bulls, and this is breeding season. That's the real reason the hands carry rifles."

She didn't know if his clarification made her feel less concerned about Jonas's safety or not. "Being either trampled or eaten doesn't seem like much of a choice."

Ryan tapped his fingers on her knee. "There's a bigger problem to deal with. I have nowhere to sleep until the carpet is cleaned and the window is fixed."

"I see where your problem is headed," she said. "This house is enormous. You don't have any other spare bed-rooms?"

"I do, but none are furnished."

He said it with a straight face, meeting her eyes all the while, and yet somehow, she suspected him of twisting a situation to his advantage—not that it mattered. They were both well aware, especially after this morning, that they'd be sleeping together while she was here. The only detail not predetermined was for how much of the night.

The entirety of it, as it turned out—at least until he got

the window replaced.

She hadn't planned to discuss her suspicions about Jonas with Ryan, but if Jonas was going to continue on in this manner, maybe she should. He might well end up fixing the Endeavour's fences for the rest of his life if she didn't.

"I believe," she said carefully, "that Jonas might be struggling to come to terms with being gay, or maybe bisexual. He said Angel dared him to bring me the flowers. It's possible that he's trying to impress Angel, who has a reputation with regard to older women. I think Jonas might have a crush on him."

She hadn't missed the glances he'd sent Angel's way during lunch, either. She suspected Angel wasn't entirely oblivious. It might be the reason he'd egged Jonas on.

"No way."

Ryan's astonished expression was comical—in an overburdened-with-manliness kind of way.

"It's not unusual for teens have difficulty coming to terms with their sexuality, especially if it's not perceived as normal by their families and friends," she said.

"Well, yeah. But do they all act like assholes?"

"More than you'd think. It would explain his overreaction to getting cut from the football team if he saw it as a slight to his manhood. Setting fire to the garage was likely in retaliation for disappointing his father, who played on a varsity team. This is all hypothetical, of course."

"Of course." Ryan sighed. "I didn't expect to have to

deal with relationship drama when I agreed to start up a group home."

"You don't have to deal with it. It's up to his counselor and me."

"I don't like you dealing with it, either."

She could see him thinking up ways to remove her from the situation and she wouldn't allow it. He had to trust her to do her job despite any slight missteps.

"Ace and Colin deal with the boys directly. My job is to provide guidance," she reminded him. "Don't forget that they're here because they have redeemable qualities. They deserve a second chance."

"I haven't forgotten." He bounced to his feet. "Speaking of second chances... Come on. Handy needs a map of the new fields they'll be fencing. Grab a warm jacket and wear sturdy boots. Nothing with heels. We're going up in the helicopter."

While that sounded like a whole lot more fun than reviewing her research, they'd agreed to maintain their distance outside of the bedroom and she had to question why her presence was required. "Why me?"

"I need someone to take notes."

When she examined his motives, she could find nothing ulterior. She was the least busy person on staff at the moment. Orphan numbers were dwindling and no new babies had been added in recent days. While happy they remained with their mothers, the end of a chore she enjoyed was clearly in sight and there had been no talk of her being given another.

Until now.

"I don't know anything about mapping," she said.

"There's no exam. All you have to do is write down the numbers I give you."

Which sounded easy enough.

They took one of the ranch's half-ton trucks to the small county airport nearby, where she'd made her initial arrival in Grand for her interview two months ago. It was the middle of May, and with the temperature a balmy seventy-three degrees, the warm jacket seemed overkill.

Ryan towed the Bell 206L LongRanger light helicopter out of one of the hangars. It seated seven, but the passenger seats folded to make room for long loads.

"It doubles as an air ambulance in emergencies," he'd told her when he'd flown her to Billings after her interview. "Technically, it belongs to the Endeavour's search and rescue operations, which fall under Dan's umbrella. I have to book it through him before I take it up."

She waited in the passenger seat while he performed a series of safety checks, then found out how cold May could get as soon as they entered the sky and Ryan circled above the airstrip. Her stomach swirled as the helicopter tipped to its side on the turn, but her half-eaten lunch remained where it belonged. When she looked through the window, she saw the Endeavour Ranch below them and the rooftops of Grand in the distance.

After a few minutes the cabin began to warm up. They wore headsets with microphones to combat the noise of the blades and she adjusted her headset so it fit more comfortably over her ears.

"How many acres of land does the ranch own?" she asked, mostly to take her mind off her stomach, so she wasn't prepared for the answer.

"A hundred and fifteen thousand. That's roughly one hundred and eighty square miles. We're not the largest operation Montana has to offer, not yet, but we're far from the smallest."

"A hundred and eighty square miles…" She tried to wrap her brain around that. It wasn't as big as all of Chicago, but it was close. "What does someone do with that much land?"

"I can't speak for other outfits, but the Endeavour raises beef, alfalfa, and a variety of grains," Ryan said. He tapped the notebook on her lap. "Montana is mostly open range, which is why ranchers brand their livestock. We're only planning to fence the parcels of land we want to keep cattle away from, in case you're worried about how much mapping we'll do today. We won't do the whole ranch."

The wild vastness of Montana beyond the Endeavour became more apparent from the sky. Badlands and plains stretched forever in all directions, cut in pieces by long stretches of the Tongue and the Yellowstone rivers. Grand sat on the junction where the two glittering ribbons of water connected. Mountains in the distance appeared a lot closer than they did from the ground.

They circled the ranch for several hours, with Ryan firing information at her while she scribbled it all down as best she could.

"Let's take a closer look at the badlands," he said through the headset when they were done.

Badlands were mini deserts that formed after vegetation was destroyed, either through overgrazing or wildfire. Water runoff and wind caused erosion, cutting soft bedrock into beautiful standing sculptures with names such as toadstools, castles, cathedrals, and balancing rocks.

"Amazing," Elizabeth breathed, wide-eyed. She'd never seen anything like it. "What are those?" She pointed to a few moving bumps on the side of a hill.

"Bighorn sheep. You'll spot elk here sometimes, too. And deer, the occasional coyote, maybe some antelope." He paused, fiddled with one of the instruments in front of him, then cast a quick glance her way. "But there aren't any bears in the area right now. I usually do a quick flyover of the ranch every few weeks and that's one of the things I check for, especially when the men are working in the fields, to make sure. No one likes to lose cattle, let alone a hand. I'm definitely not about to lose one of the kids, no matter how big a pain in the ass Jonas might be. I agreed to take on a group home for boys because I used to be Jonas. Except for the potentially gay part, of course."

"Of course."

A smile smoothed out the faint cleft in his chin. "But I was angry, aggressive, and afraid. Anyone who tried to get close to me had to prove I could trust them. That's how I became friends with Dan and Dallie, you know. I took these two underage country boys I'd barely just met to a bar that didn't check ID too closely, then stole a police car on the walk home. All because I wanted their friendship. They were either in with me or they were out. They both stuck by me, as hard as that is to believe—although Dan kicked my ass for it later. That ass kicking was totally earned." He shot her another quick glance. The smile slipped a little. Became serious. "I'm sorry about lunch."

Her heart bobbed up and down in her chest in a manner that went far beyond fluttering, then began a slow slide into unfamiliar, unexpected, uncharted territory. When he decided an apology was in order, he went about it in a big way. She could take lessons.

"Me too," she said.

Ryan

ONCE A WEEK, the Endeavour's owners sat down to go over their business.

Initially, they'd met in the common area of the main

house. With the growing number of people who lived at the ranch, and the increased likelihood of interruption, they'd gradually shifted those meetings to the garage, where one of Ryan's cars served as their office.

He owned two Mercedes AMGs—a black one as well as his favorite, the steel blue. Those were the everyday cars. He also owned a Ferrari 488 Spider, custom-painted in British racing-car green, and a bright red Jaguar XE. Dan sometimes took the Jag to the Grand Dragstrip Racetrack and let Jazz heat up the tires whenever she needed to burn off some stress. According to Roman, the racetrack's owner and chief driving instructor, she was a natural.

Dallas liked the black AMG. He said the grill on the front made it look like Tom Hardy as Bane in one of the Batman movies, which pretty much ruined it for Ryan, because now he couldn't unsee it.

The black AMG was where they were conducting their business. Ryan sat in the driver's seat, as usual, with Dan riding shotgun and Dallas flopped in back. Dan and Dallas moved through their reports much more quickly than he did. Jazz wrote Dan's for him and Dallas had an office manager who took care of his, whereas Ryan preferred to take care of his own.

He plowed through his update on the group home and the ranch's financial statements, and had started in on the rodeo's progress report, when Dan interrupted.

"When are you planning to hand the rodeo's management over to Miles?" he asked.

In his head, Ryan said *never*. Out loud, he was less frank. Every time he was honest with these guys, they tag-teamed him and put his plans to a vote. And every time, he came out the loser. That was how he'd ended up hiring Miles in the first place. Elizabeth too, although he had fewer complaints about that every day.

"In the new year," he replied vaguely. Dan was good at being a sheriff and had a bullshit detector that worked better than most. Ryan never lied to him outright, although he didn't always tell him the whole truth. In return, Dan picked his battles.

Dan blew out a breath—half exasperation, half resignation—which meant he was willing to let this battle slide for the moment. "Don't forget that Miles only hired on because we agreed he could run things his way."

"You've got a lot on the go. Maybe you should give up on the rodeo if you don't want Miles to run it for you," Dallas suggested, jumping in with his opinion. "It wasn't a requirement of the bequest, was it?"

That stupid bequest. He and Judge Palmeter had agreed the fewer people who knew the details surrounding it the better, including Dallas and Dan, to keep the Adriana Gallants of the world from digging too deep. His friends knew part of his history. They didn't need to know everything, though. The world didn't, either. Giaco Cienetti Tosaro was dead. Long live Ryan O'Connell.

"It wasn't," Ryan said, even though the question was rhetorical because Dallas was fully aware that the rodeo was intended to generate revenue for ranching operations. "But it will benefit Grand too, don't forget."

"I haven't forgotten." Dallas hung an elbow on the back of the front passenger seat and leaned into the space between Ryan and Dan. His lips pressed into a straight line and curled slightly inward, signaling he'd had a thought of the utmost importance. "I'd like to talk about the requirements around our living arrangements, though."

"What's wrong with our living arrangements?" He'd put plenty of effort into them, and couldn't imagine better options, but Dallas and Dan both eyeballed him as if he'd said something dumb.

Dan answered first. "There was nothing wrong with them while we were all single. So far, it's been great. But now we have women to factor into our lives and I doubt if they'll like sharing their space as much as we do."

"The units are all self-contained. They each have their own patio, too." He knew he sounded defensive, but seriously. The ranch house was enormous, and the units were actual apartments. Calling it shared space was borderline insulting. Jazz shared living quarters with firefighters. No privacy there. And Hannah lived above her brewery with a parking lot for a backyard.

"Don't get your panties bunched in a wad," Dallas said, patting his shoulder. "Have you asked Elizabeth for her opinion?"

"Why would I do that?"

"Was he always this stupid?" Dallas asked Dan.

"Because you're living together," Dan said to Ryan, his mild manner, so misleading to others, intimating that his answer to Dallas's question was yes.

Ryan wasn't ready to discuss his relationship with Elizabeth with them. He liked living with her, and not just for the sex, although he liked that a lot, too. It was peaceful to sit on the sofa with her in the evenings while she worked on her dissertation and he ran through the ranch's accounts. She brought stability to his life—a balance, of sorts—that he'd never had. Her presence made his house feel like a real home.

"We are right now, sure, but who knows how long it will last?" he replied.

"How long do you want it to last?"

Another good question on Dan's part. One he'd been avoiding himself. Elizabeth wanted to work at the group home so she could finish her dissertation. He couldn't say what her plans were beyond that. Maybe he didn't want to know.

Maybe he did.

Dallas leaped in. Again. "Then there's always the matter of kids. I don't know about you guys, but Hannah and I are going to have eight."

"Way to help ease the burden of global overpopulation," Dan congratulated him, momentarily diverted.

Eight. Didn't that number boggle the mind? To think Ryan worried about one. "I'll do my part by not having any."

Dallas and Dan, the bastards, looked at each other and burst into laughter.

"Afraid that's not all up to you, buddy," Dallas said.

No worries there. "Elizabeth doesn't want any, either."

"You sure about that?"

Ryan recalled her horror over the condom incident and her quick trip to Family Planning to take care of the problem. "Positive."

Dallas appeared a whole lot less convinced. "If you say so."

"I do."

Elizabeth was as practical as he was. Thanks to the group home, he could see her sliding easily into his life on the ranch on a permanent basis. He'd have to find a good time for them to discuss it.

Just not yet.

Not until he was certain of her feelings for him.

Chapter Twelve

Elizabeth

THE FINAL TWO boys arrived the last week in June, filling the group home to capacity. Ryan charged into Elizabeth's office one morning soon after.

"I'm about to head out on one of the ATVs to check on how the breeding program is doing," he said. "Want to come with me?"

She'd heard a lot about the breeding program over the past month or so, and she knew the Endeavour was working toward a sixty-day season, but they hadn't yet hit that goal. She'd witnessed the first phase, which was artificial insemination, because AI—as it was known—was easier to track and had a higher fertility rate. The larger and older bulls on the ranch were used for cleanup toward the end of the season, meaning any cows that came into heat after they should have been bred.

"Don't the bulls know what they're doing?" she asked.

"For the most part." The cleft in his chin flickered along with his grin. "But Miles is conducting some genetic research for a program he's running, which means taking samples, plus we have to vaccinate and deworm them before we can turn them loose on the ladies. Handling bulls requires as many men as we can spare. Colin and Ace are taking the kids."

"That doesn't sound safe."

"They get to move gates around to help contain them. They don't get to ride them."

"I'd better come along to make sure they don't do anything stupid," she said. "We're talking teenaged boys. You know someone is going to dare someone else to do exactly that." Besides, fresh air would be good. She'd been working long hours, and lately, had begun to feel the effect.

"I'LL MEET YOU outside the machine shed in ten minutes."

Elizabeth ran to change into boots and jeans, then joined Ryan at the machine shed. The ranch owned six ATVs and four half-ton trucks, because for the most part, machines were more practical than horses. They sometimes used the helicopter for roundup, but not if they had to land close to the cattle. The trucks and two of the ATVs were already gone.

"Do you want your own or do you want to ride with me?" Ryan asked.

"I'll ride with you."

She hadn't had motion sickness since she was a little girl, but bouncing through the fields on the back of an ATV brought back old memories, none of them fond. By the time they reached their destination, she'd made up her mind to ride home in one of the trucks.

Nineteen bulls, weighing between two thousand and twenty-five hundred pounds each, waited with growing impatience. They looked like cattle on steroids when compared to the more delicate ladies. Muscle bulged across their shoulders and necks. One end of their pasture had been fenced off and metal gates, to be used as hand-held chutes by the men to force the bulls into the makeshift corral, sprawled on the ground, ready for action.

Boys swung their legs from truck tailgates and lolled on the ground, waiting to be told what to do. One of them hung from the wire fence, waving at the bulls to attract their attention, until Colin grabbed him by the collar of his shirt and dragged him away.

Colin dumped the boy next to one of the trucks. "What did I tell you guys?" he demanded. "You don't think that fence will hold those beasts back if you wind them up, do you?"

Elizabeth was certainly no expert, but that didn't sound safe.

"Go sit in the back of one of the trucks and watch," Ryan said to her. "That way I know where you are."

"Do you really think the boys are going to be of any

use?"

"None whatsoever," he replied cheerfully. "Except maybe Jonas. He's been out in the fields and sort of knows what to expect."

The day proved enlightening as well as uneventful. The bulls weren't only vaccinated and dewormed. They were sprayed for flies and had their penises disinfected. None of it made them happy.

The boys did their part by holding the gates to the chute. Elizabeth's lungs forgot how to function when the first irritable bull approached them, but the boys used their gates as barriers, and the bull obediently veered away and into the narrow chute opening. The same for the next.

The more experienced ranch hands took care of the treatments. Ryan and Miles supervised.

Ryan was the one who hoarded her attention. He hadn't bothered wearing a hat. Dark glasses kept the sun out of his eyes. He'd rolled up his sleeves. Jeans strained over muscular thighs as he squatted to lift one of the metal kits containing the medication. Lust, interlaced with affection, jacked up her heart. He'd be easy to love, if she wasn't more careful.

But working together as well as sharing their private space continued to wave bright red flags. They hadn't yet had their first fight, and how they handled the fallout remained to be seen.

He caught her staring at him. Black Bart emerged, reminding her of what they'd been doing earlier, before they got out of bed, and she felt herself blush. This was the one area of their relationship that wasn't complicated at all—except it caused all the complications.

By suppertime, she'd been out in the sun for most of the day, and as a result, had a headache. She reconsidered riding home in one of the pickups with the boys. Cutting across country through the fields would be faster. She wouldn't have to listen to them, either.

She climbed onto the ATV, hugged Ryan around the waist, and warmed her cheek against his solid back. He smelled of clean sweat and fresh air, and she closed her eyes so she could enjoy it.

The return ride turned out better than expected after her morning experience, likely because he employed a more leisurely pace. They stopped once so he could show her three killdeer hatchlings nested on a low, rocky crest.

Even so, they were first to arrive at the machine shop, with Handy and Steve close behind on the other two ATVs.

"There's slow cooker chili in the cookhouse," Ryan said, holding her elbow to steady her while she dismounted. He'd ditched the dark glasses. They peeped out of his breast pocket. "Give me a sec to hang up the keys and refill the gas tank, then we can eat."

She tried to imagine eating a bowlful of chili. "I'll pass and maybe grab some soup and a salad at the house."

He paused, keys in his hand and concern in his eyes. "You okay?"

She wanted so much to kiss him, but he'd take a mile if given an inch and the ranch had eyes everywhere. She would never have believed she'd fall for a man as possessive as this one, but when she looked in his eyes and saw the way he looked back, her lungs flipped upside down and tickled her belly so hard she forgot why she had reservations.

So *easy to love...*

"Too much sun."

Halfway to the house, a rogue wave of nausea swelled up from nowhere and she stopped and threw up in one of the bushes. She made it as far as the bedroom before her stomach turned over again. She dashed for the bathroom and made it with seconds to spare.

Afterward, when she deemed it was safe, she wiped her face on a fluffy white towel and stared at her face in the mirror. The dark shadows under her eyes, and pale, sickly skin, made her look like a character out of a *Twilight* movie. She did some mental math but the numbers were off. She hoped her uneasy stomach and poor mathematical skills were both due to sunstroke.

Otherwise, this was an incredibly unfortunate turn of events.

SHE DROVE TO the drugstore in a neighboring town the next day after work, because the last thing she wanted was for word to spread around Grand that she'd bought a pregnancy test.

She couldn't be pregnant.

She didn't *want* to be pregnant.

Her family was so emotionally dysfunctional, she'd decided a long time ago that she didn't want someone in her life with the same baggage as hers. That someone was Ryan.

But she might have been fine with not having children with him.

Clamminess coated her skin. She'd taken the morning-after pill. She hadn't been in the danger zone as far as ovulation went, or so she'd assumed, but so many things could alter hormonal rhythms. A change in diet was one of them, and the food served by teens in the cookhouse was a definite change in her regular eating habits. She'd never be able to eat pizza again. The thought of it had her contemplating pulling the car over so she could be sick.

She made it to the parking lot and entered the drugstore through gleaming glass doors that parted with a guttural protest upon her approach. The blast of air-conditioned interior air was welcome, and did a lot toward calming her nerves and her stomach.

She found the right aisle and stared at the numerous products on the shelves. She couldn't decide which test would be the most accurate, so she grabbed three different brands. At the checkout, she placed the three boxes on the counter.

"Congratulations, dear," the clerk said, smiling broadly as she rang them through as if a monumental disaster wasn't unfolding right in front of her face. "Your baby is going to be beautiful if he takes after his mama."

A conversation like this would never take place in Chicago. All Elizabeth could respond with was, "Thanks."

She grabbed her bag and tried not to run on her way to the car.

The half hour return trip to the ranch was the longest she'd ever endured, but finally, she made it. She barreled through the main door, intent on getting the tests over with before Ryan returned from a full day of business meetings in Billings. He'd taken the helicopter and planned to be home before bedtime.

She collided with Dallas, who was trying to exit as she blundered in, and clipped his chin with the top of her skull. The bag flew from her hand and its contents spewed free to skid across the stone floor.

"Whoa," Dallas said. He rubbed his chin. "Sorry about that."

Elizabeth stooped to pick up a pregnancy test lodged against his foot but he got to it first. He scooped up the now-empty bag, too.

He looked at the two items he held in his hands. He focused on the pregnancy test for a second. Silence stretched to the arched ceiling, expanding that second to hours. He looked at the other two bright, neon boxes, blazing guiltily on the floor where she'd dropped them. Finally, he looked at Elizabeth. The redheaded curse scoured her cheeks.

He picked up the remaining two tests, placed them in the bag with the first, then handed the whole ticking time bomb to her.

"I'm here if you need to talk," he said, proving he wasn't nearly as oblivious as his reputation suggested.

She clutched the bag to her chest and blinked soggy lashes. She longed to take him up on his offer. Kindness glowed like a halo around him. She had no one else to turn to in Grand and he was a doctor. Who better to talk to?

But he was also one of Ryan's closest friends and she didn't want to make trouble between them. "Won't that put you in an awkward position?"

"You have no idea. But it's too late to worry about it. The pregnancy test—tests—are out of the bag. One would have been plenty, by the way. Say… Why don't we take care of this right now? Morning would be best, because that's when hCG levels are most concentrated, but since you've got three tests, if the results are uncertain, you can always try again tomorrow, and sorry, I'm babbling. Follow me."

He gently steered her toward the door of his suite and she allowed herself to be led.

Dallas's home was laid out with much the same floor plan as Ryan's, although flipped around. They entered a tiny vestibule that opened into the living room, which was identical, but the door to the bedrooms fell to the right, not the left. He opened the door to the right and showed her to a small powder room directly across the hall. He hovered outside it, concern in his posture.

"Need me to read the instructions for you?" he asked.

Her brain had quit working, so that might be best. "Please."

He walked her through the instructions, which were fairly straightforward despite her muddled state, then left her alone. She took the first test, waited, and after the requisite amount of minutes had passed according to the clock on her phone, stared at the results.

Positive.

She opened the second test with numb fingers and fumbled through the new set of instructions.

Dallas tapped on the door. "Everything okay in there?"

She tried to breathe. To sound normal. To keep it together. Because the second test was positive, too.

"I'm fine," she said.

"Let me know if you need anything."

She needed for this to not be happening.

She crumpled onto the floor with her arms folded across her bent knees and her forehead on her arms and cried deep, silent sobs. She couldn't say for how long, but it must have been long enough for Dallas to worry, because he knocked again.

"Open the door, Elizabeth," he said, speaking through the wood panel.

"Just a minute."

She washed her face, which didn't create much of an improvement if the mirror was any judge, then unlocked the door. Dallas leaned against the wall with his hands in his pockets. He wore a white business shirt and navy trousers, meaning he must have been on his way to the hospital, since clinic hours were over for the day.

"I'm keeping you from work," she said, stricken by guilt. He'd waited while she took two pregnancy tests—he was right, three were too many—when he had patients waiting who likely needed him more.

"I called. Outpatients is quiet and one of the other doctors said she'd stick around until I come in. Let's go sit down so we can talk." *Before you fall down*, his expression added.

Out in the living room, Elizabeth sank into an enormous brown leather chair. Dallas took the sofa across from it. He crossed one leg over the other knee, clasped his hands on his thigh, and went into full doctor mode while he waited for her to sort out her thoughts.

"How am I going to tell Ryan?" she finally asked, trying to disguise the wild hitch of alarm in her voice by clearing her throat.

Hazel eyes examined her with compassion from under a tangle of glossy black curls that always seemed badly in need of a trim. "Let's not worry about Ryan just yet. First, how do you feel about it?"

Her head ached from crying, and now, she couldn't

think. She massaged her forehead with the back of her hand. "Like the timing couldn't be worse. Like I hadn't planned for this to happen."

"I gathered all of that. But if you had planned for it, what would be different about it?"

What a ridiculous question. "*Everything.*"

Dallas, however, appeared to be leading her somewhere specific. "Including the father?"

And there it was. Her headache spread to her toes. "Ryan's not exactly father material."

But what if he were?

What then?

"I see." Dallas frowned. "Is that your professional or personal opinion?"

Neither. It was a gut feeling, possibly brought on by her fear of the unknown. "Both."

"If that's your honest and unbiased opinion, then you have to consider your options. Decisions will need to be made as to what the next eighteen to twenty years of your life will look like. Maybe you should give yourself a few days to think about what you want before you tell him about the baby."

Baby.

The word put a whole different spin on this turn of events. It went so far beyond pregnancy, which a physical state. Her palm smoothed over her stomach, where the slightest of bumps had started to form, another consequence of being short—or possibly because she was bloated by water retention thanks to an overabundance of hormones. Either way, she had a new life growing inside her.

The wonder she'd felt when she witnessed her first calf being born was nothing compared to the wonder overwhelming her now. The practical part of her brain said to get used to the mood swings because there'd be plenty more where that came from. The hormonal part attached itself to the room's wagon wheel chandelier and swayed like a drunken frat boy at a house party.

"But before you do anything you might regret later," Dallas continued, oblivious to the battle her hormones were waging, so his reputation might be partially deserved, "how about if I give you my personal opinion—as Ryan's friend—first? He had a rough childhood. He learned to lie to protect himself early on, and he's still dodgy with the truth when it comes to something he wants, but Dan and I trust him completely. He doesn't let too many people get close to him, but when he does, he stands by them. He commits one hundred percent. He'll do anything for them. And he's let you get closer to him than even Dan and I are. You'll never find a guy who'll make a better father—although you might have to work on his control issues a little." He'd get no argument there. "The problem is that he won't know how great he'll be at it until he tries, and he's not going to try unless you make him."

Dallas was probably right about that, too. How could a

man who helped bring new animal life into the world with such care possibly object to one tiny new human he'd helped create?

But Elizabeth wasn't about to make Ryan do anything he didn't want. Not even the crazy hormones currently trashing Dallas's home could change her mind about that. Despite knowing Ryan wasn't who she'd planned on for sharing her life, she'd fallen in love with him, which meant accepting his faults. He and the baby were now two separate issues and she'd have to deal with them in two separate ways.

"I'll take everything you said under advisement." She pried the frat boy off the chandelier and herself from the chair. Dallas stood too. Impulsively, she threw her arms around him. "Thank you."

Dallas hugged her back. "Anything for a friend."

Chapter Thirteen

Ryan

R ANCH WORK DIDN'T halt for holidays. Ryan gave everyone the afternoon of the Fourth of July off, anyway.

The counselors had taken their charges to the swimming hole in the Tongue River for a few hours. Two propane barbecues had been set up in the outdoor kitchen on the Endeavour's back lawn. Elizabeth, pretty in a blue sundress and sandals, with her red curls in a high ponytail that brushed her cheek whenever she bent her head forward, laid out condiments, salads, and sweets on a skirted buffet table.

She insisted on maintaining a level of formality between them outside of the bedroom. Meanwhile, he took advantage of every opportunity that presented itself to remind her they were living together. It had turned into a game. A fun one.

But she'd been distracted for the past week and he wanted to know why.

He dropped a quick kiss on her cheek as he walked by, catching a tormenting whiff of the almond-scented sunscreen she'd slathered herself with in the process. The sun caught the amber in her eyes and turned them to gold. She smiled for him, spreading lightness and warmth through his chest.

The subject of the future hadn't come up yet. He was thinking about how to approach it, though.

He'd never seen himself settled down, and he definitely didn't see himself turning into a family man, not like Dan and Dallas, but since Elizabeth was so focused on her career, there was a good chance a traditional family life might not be all that important to her.

He wasn't quite ready to discuss it. They'd only known each other for three months. They'd been living together for less than two of them.

But he was definitely thinking about it.

Hannah tapped him on the shoulder. Dan and Dallas both had the day free, so she and Jazz had shown up to help out with the cooking.

"The sixer is in Dallas's kitchen," Hannah said. A sixer was a small keg that held forty-two pints. "That seemed the safest way to keep it from tempting the kids." She liked to experiment with new recipes for her brewery by trying them out on her friends, so she'd brought a smoked porter with jalapenos for the adults to taste.

Elizabeth's face paled. Her hand flew to her mouth. "I don't think I can drink that."

"You won't hurt my feelings," Hannah reassured her, her pretty face sincere. "Not everyone likes beer, and a porter is an acquired taste."

"Especially a smoked porter with jalapenos," Ryan added. Anticipation didn't sing through his veins either, even
though he'd never tried one of Hannah's experiments to date
that wasn't top notch. She had great instincts when it came
to her craft.

He spotted Owen racing up the path from the bunkhouses, waving his arms. His first fear was that someone had
drowned. He didn't wait for Owen to come to him, but
began running toward him. Elizabeth was running too, but
he quickly outpaced her.

"Fight," Owen panted out when they met, pointing behind him. Outside the horse barn. "Ace said to get you."

Ryan charged around the barn at full throttle to find Ace
holding Angel in a headlock and Colin with Jonas's arms
pinned behind him.

"What's going on here?" he demanded.

Whatever it was, Jonas had come out ahead. A few
months of fencing had given him serious muscle.

"He called me a faggot," Jonas said, his voice high and
angry and his entire body quivering. He kicked out at Angel
with both feet, causing Colin to stagger as he tried to carry
Jonas's full weight.

"I did not," Angel protested, red-faced. He had a bruise
building under one eye. "I was politically correct. I told him
to quit acting so gay."

Ryan was overjoyed to leave it to the counselors to deal

with whatever had brought on that particular request. "Let them go."

As soon as Ace let go, Jonas lunged for Angel, but Ryan was ready. He hooked him around the upper body with both arms, hauling him back.

"You and me," Ryan said. "Let's go blow off some steam."

Elizabeth had arrived by now, slightly out of breath from running, going all case manager and business on them, which would have been funny if tempers weren't raging. The cute ponytail didn't lend her a whole lot of credibility in this particular crowd.

"I don't think that's a good idea," she said.

"It's an excellent idea," Ryan assured her. Her level of confidence in him was flattering. "I'm not going to kill him." Although a little fear might do Jonas some good.

He marched the boy toward one of the farm trucks and hustled him into the passenger seat. "Stay there. Don't move. If I have to chase you, it won't put me in a good mood."

"Where are you taking me?" Jonas asked. He slumped in his seat, doing as he was told, but not hiding how he felt about it. Wariness warred with belligerence.

"You'll see."

Elizabeth, who'd followed, wedged herself between Ryan and the driver's side door. "I'm coming, too."

"Suit yourself."

He boosted her into the cab before climbing in after her.

They weren't going far. He drove the ten miles to the airport, bumped the old truck down a dirt road that parted two fields, then pulled up next to one of the hangars.

"Wait here," he said. He eyed Elizabeth, who'd pokered up as if prepared to fight to the death to protect Jonas from him, which seemed unfair, since he hadn't started the rumble with Angel. "Break his leg if he does anything you don't like," he said, to annoy her a bit more. "I'll break the other one when I get back."

"No one is breaking anyone's legs," she reassured Jonas, making Ryan wonder whose side she was on.

He entered the hangar, which housed the smoke jumper base that Jazz ran, and grabbed a key from the wall next to her office. He jotted his name on the sign-out sheet. He returned to the truck, where Elizabeth and Jonas both clammed up when they saw him. Whatever they were discussing, they didn't want him to hear it. No problem. He'd get it out of her later.

"Let's go," he said.

He led them across the tarmac to a hangar on the far side. The ranch had built an obstacle course that Jazz and the firefighters used for training. He'd planned on bringing the kids to check it out over the winter, but right now, during the fire season, it was technically off-limits.

Bright pinks, blues, and yellows, assaulted the eyes when they entered. The course sprawled from one end of the hangar to the other, and towered in places. Thick mats padded the floor. A simulated helicopter fuselage, some fifty feet overhead, could only be accessed by a zipline from above or the knotted rope dangling from the platform to the ground.

"Dope," Jonas breathed, his head swiveling to take it all in.

Ryan peeled off his shirt and kicked off his shoes. "Handy tells me you're a good worker. He says you're tough. You want to prove you're tough to the world, this is the best way to do it, because there's nobody tougher than smoke-jumpers. They run this course in full firefighting gear. Fighting just proves you're an asshole."

He picked up a stopwatch that hung next to the training gear and tossed it to Elizabeth. "You can time us to keep it fair. I'll go first to show him how it's done. He beats me, he can call it quits with the fencing. I beat him, he apologizes to Angel. Deal?" he said, turning to Jonas.

"Deal."

Jonas's eagerness as he examined the course was almost painful to see. It told Ryan he should have taken more of an interest, not only in Jonas, but all of the boys. They were all misfits, same as he'd once been, which was why they were here—but they each had their own talents and strengths, and the Endeavour was the perfect place to help sort them out.

"You can take as many tries as you need. Only the helicopter is off-limits," Ryan said. "Jazz won't allow anyone but the smokejumpers to climb fifty feet." He squared off at the start and nodded at Elizabeth. "Ready."

There were ten obstacles in all. The first was a glaring pink rope bridge, stretched across twenty feet of red matting. The purpose was to cling to it upside down and shimmy across underneath. Next up came horizontal cargo netting, meant to be crawled under, then a vertical net, which had to be climbed.

Ryan slowed a fraction at the tire obstacle, leaping with precision from one to the other, then swung across the monkey bars, taking a few seconds longer than he should. He cleared the next wall and eased back on the throttle again. He crossed the balance beam, wobbling with a complete lack of grace, before ending the course with a stump hop an old man could beat.

"Your turn," he puffed to Jonas, resting his hands on his thighs to give his lungs a chance to catch up. The course was a lot harder than it looked. Otherwise, what was the point?

Jonas swung into action. He must have paid close attention, because the only obstacle that caused him any real trouble was the pink rope bridge at the very first of the course. The hard work of fencing had gone a long way toward physical endurance, too. Ryan almost wished he hadn't spotted him those extra few seconds.

Jonas jogged up to Elizabeth, eager to hear how he'd done.

"You won by four seconds," she said, delighted.

"You don't have to sound so happy about it," Ryan said.

He clapped Jonas on the shoulder. "Congratulations. No more fencing for you."

"Oh, I'm sticking with the fencing," Jonas assured him, red-faced from spent energy and beaming with pride. "But I'm not apologizing to Angel. He's still a dick."

JONAS HOPPED FROM the truck before it had rolled to a complete stop, but he headed for the horse barn instead of the barbecue. Since he wasn't in the right frame of mind to socialize yet, Ryan let him go.

Elizabeth remained where she was, with her thigh pressed tight against his. Her eyes smiled up at him in a way he particularly liked. It made him feel special. It told him she was his, whether or not she said it out loud.

He loved her. He knew it as surely as he knew the sun rose in the east. He loved the way she bossed him around. He loved how she doubted him, and yet always seemed to believe he meant to do the right thing—even those times when he didn't. She ranked his motives higher than his actions.

And she looked at him right now as if she really believed he was a far better man than he was. Which only served to make her distance the past little while all that more perplexing. He wished he could be as confident of her feelings as he was of his own.

"You let him win," she said. The afternoon sun caught her eyes.

"You tacked on two extra seconds."

"Did not."

"Did too."

"Maybe I did." She took his hand. "Maybe I'll make it up to you later."

He folded her delicate, fine-boned fingers protectively into his work-hardened palm. Maybe it wasn't too soon to discuss the future with her, after all. If they had a problem, he had to know. Better sooner than later.

"You can make it up to me now. Come with me."

He hopped from the truck and lifted her down. She was so tiny, and yet such a force, the same as the blizzard she'd blown into his life on. He reclaimed her hand and led her up the path toward the garage, not the house. The garage was the one place where they could talk uninterrupted.

She followed him willingly enough, but not without a whole string of questions. "Now? Shouldn't we head back to the barbecue? Aren't you supposed to be in charge of it?"

"Do you really think Dan and Dallie can't handle a few boys?"

"Fair. At least tell me why we're going to the garage."

"To see my car collection."

She balked again, dragging her heels. "We're not having sex in the back seat of one of your cars. You have security cameras everywhere in there."

Which pretty much meant if not for those cameras, she'd give it serious consideration. "I know how to turn them off. But sex in the back seat of a car isn't what I have planned." Although of course now, he couldn't get the possibility out of his head.

They reached the garage. He punched in the code and unlocked the side door. Inside, natural light flooded the showroom floor from a skylight above. The steel-blue AMG was where Ryan pondered life and all its odd little turns. Sometimes he never left the garage. He wasn't planning to leave it now. This was a sit-and-chat kind of talk, not the drive-and-think, escape-from-it-all variety.

He opened the passenger door. "Have a seat. I want to talk to you."

"Can't it wait?"

"Sure. But admit it. You're dying to find out what I want to talk about."

"I am." She got in the car, releasing another barrage of questions. "Why do we have to talk here? Why not the house or the office?" Her face took on an expression of horror. Amber eyes lit up in preparation for battle. "Are you *firing* me? Is that why we're here? Because you don't want any witnesses if I make a scene?"

He rubbed his head. "Jesus, Elizabeth. I'm not firing you. We had an agreement. You've got almost three months left before I can do that. I wanted to discuss us living together."

She got more comfortable, bending one knee and tucking it under her skirt, so she could face him. One hand rested on the car's dash. The other, the back of her seat. "Technically, we're not living together."

"Technically, yes, we are." It amused him that she still argued about it. "But that's not what's important. Where do you see yourself in five years?"

She tilted her head as she considered the question. "What's this really about?"

He couldn't quite put his finger on it, but something about the way she'd responded seemed… off. "I like what we have. I like you working in the office next to mine. I like you living with me. I'm curious if the group home will be enough for you." *If I'll be enough.*

"So, you aren't planning to fire me in three months?"

"No. But you've been a little distracted lately. I'm curious what's wrong."

"I'm not sure how you'll take it." She didn't meet his eyes, which wasn't like her at all.

He began to wish he'd left things alone. Maybe he wasn't enough for her. She could definitely do better.

"There's only one way to find out. Hit me with it."

"I'm pregnant."

Elizabeth

SHE WATCHED HIM closely. Incomprehension came first, then, the news hit home. Something in his eyes died. A blank screen dropped into place.

She'd certainly hit him with it. And hard.

"That's not possible," he said.

"Three positive pregnancy tests suggest otherwise."

"That's pretty strong evidence, alright." He stared at the dash for a second, as if clearing his thoughts, before looking at her. "Is that what's been bothering you?" He said it as if her news wasn't a problem at all, but his eyes told her he lied. "You'd be, what—only seven, maybe eight weeks along? There's a clinic in Billings, although I'd prefer to pay for a private doctor. Either way, you don't have to go through this alone. I'll be right there with you the whole time."

She couldn't make sense of his words. "What are you talking about?"

"Abortions are legal in Montana. This isn't a big deal."

"I don't want an abortion." She'd never entertained it as a possibility. "I don't want a baby right now either, but it's too late. The future's been decided. This baby is happening."

"Not if we take care of it. The sooner, the better."

Elizabeth felt ill. "This is our *baby* we're talking about."

"No, we're talking about a cluster of cells."

The news was as upsetting for him as it had been for her, and she'd had longer to process it. She was terrified she'd say something she might come to regret. But she was the one with a new life growing inside her—a life that was wholly dependent on her for survival. She was the one who'd have to put her career on hold. And she was the one willing to make the sacrifices required. She'd hoped he'd be willing to support her decisions.

She struggled to remain pragmatic and not give in to emotion. "You once told me you didn't believe I had it in me to break someone's leg, even if my own life was in danger, and you were right. I don't have it in me. Which is why I don't have it in me to end this baby's life, either."

"It's not a baby. It's not even a fetus yet," Ryan insisted. "I'd understand if you were far enough along for it to be viable, but that's months away. I agree abortion isn't an ideal solution, but it's the only option we've got."

He'd overlooked one important detail. One she'd had to stress, in a professional capacity, herself. "*You* don't have any options," she said, gentle but firm. "I do. And for me, this is about more than whether or not a fetus is viable. It's about my body and my right to decide what I do with it."

"You want to use your body as an incubator. I get it. But those are hormones talking, Elizabeth. Not common sense." He drummed his thumb against the steering wheel, as if trying to make his mind up about something. Indecision traipsed between his mouth and his eyes. His grip on the wheel tightened. "You can't make an informed decision because you don't have the full story. Here it is. When I lived in Chicago, my name was Giaco Cienetti Tosaro. Jackie. My grandfather was Giaco Cienetti. I was named for him. My dad was Giaco's accountant, and as his son-in-law, he must have decided dipping into the petty cash was no big deal. My mother didn't seem to think it was either, but unfortunately, Giaco didn't feel the same way. He ordered the hit."

On his own son-in-law. So this was what happened to Cienetti's daughter and her family. A documentary on the Jackal had aired the night she'd gotten pregnant, she recalled. It came on the television right after the Disney princess movie they'd made the boys watch. Ryan had switched to another channel. She'd seen so many of those so-called documentaries that she'd stopped paying attention. His insistence on an abortion as the only solution made a little more sense.

"Your mother changed your names when you moved to Montana," she said, encouraging him to talk more. She wanted to understand his position as best she could. He had no say in what she did with her body. He'd have a great deal of say in what happened after the baby was born.

"She didn't change our names. They were changed for us when we entered the witness protection program. She'd given up a lot of information on Giaco. Sadly, none of it stuck. She was willing to try but figured he'd bought off too many people. And now you know why having this baby is such a bad idea."

She cradled an arm protectively over her stomach. Her heart cracked a little for him. On the surface he appeared cold and well in control of his emotions. In reality, he was operating purely on fear.

It didn't sway her resolve. An abortion was a decision they couldn't undo. "No, I'm afraid I don't."

His Adam's apple bobbed in his throat and his voice thickened. "Tell me how your family will feel about you having Giaco Cienetti's great-grandchild—not to mention, the grandchild of a mob accountant who was also an embezzler."

Her parents weren't perfect. They'd been damaged by crime, the same as him. But they weren't cold or cruel. This baby might be the best thing to happen to them since Marianne.

To Ryan, too—if she handled it right. He saw Giaco in himself. He believed Giaco would emerge in their baby. Childhood therapy likely taught him that antisocial personality disorders were hereditary.

But there was so much more to an APD diagnosis than a few traits he might share with a grandfather he'd barely known. Ryan had far too much self-control to be labeled a sociopath and lacked the charm associated with a true psychopath. His relationships with the people he loved were far from shallow. If only he could see what she and his best friends saw.

"I'm having their grandchild too," she said. "That's all

my parents will care about. It's all they'll need to know. You haven't been Jackie Cienetti Tosaro since you were seven years old."

"In a few weeks, after you've thought this through, it'll be too late to change your mind."

"I won't change my mind."

"Neither will I. I don't want to bring another Cienetti into the world and I won't be a part of it. Since it's your body and your choice, go ahead and choose. Your baby or me. Which is it?"

Your baby.

She struggled to hold it together. She hadn't expected him to be overcome with joy at the news he was going to be a father. Becoming a mother wasn't news she'd wanted, either. But she hadn't expected an ultimatum from him. A chunk of ice impaled her heart and pumped frozen slush through her veins. The chill spread from her chest to her fingers and toes.

She shouldn't be shocked. This was a man who'd once tested his friends' loyalty by convincing them to help him steal a police car. Now, he tested hers.

She wasn't a naïve teenaged boy, however. She was a pregnant adult who'd known the risks and was prepared to accept the consequences. She also had to accept the very real possibility that Ryan might never feel the same way.

But she would never, under any circumstances, hold this tiny life accountable for its family history. She spoke through numb lips.

"The baby."

She fumbled out of the car. Ryan didn't try to stop her.

Keep it together. Keep it together. Keep it together.

She couldn't lose control now.

She couldn't go back to the barbecue either, so she headed for the house. She heard the garage doors creak open behind her, followed by the rev of an engine. The AMG roared out and down the long drive and away from the ranch.

She got it. He needed space and they'd said all there was to be said for the moment. She'd have to wait until he was ready to discuss what happened next.

By two o'clock in the morning, it became clear he wasn't coming back to discuss anything anytime soon. That was when she began to face certain realities surrounding her situation.

She was a social worker, working with children, who'd gotten pregnant by her employer. She wouldn't be able to hide the pregnancy from the group home staff and its residents forever. Ryan definitely wouldn't be able to hide how he felt about it and that wasn't healthy for anyone.

While she hated having to give up on her research, and on the boys, she couldn't stay at the ranch, clinging to hope, waiting for Ryan to come to his senses. Living offsite and commuting to work was an option, although hardly ideal, and little more than a short-term solution.

She'd head back to Chicago and pick up her old life. Her career. With a few major adjustments. She'd find her own place to live. Her parents wouldn't be pleased about it, but she'd already made the break with them and they'd all begun to move forward. Her mistakes weren't going to become theirs. She had a trust fund to draw on so money wasn't a worry. She'd focus on her dissertation until the baby was born. She'd keep the lines of communication open with Ryan, in case he had a change of heart, but she had to prepare for the possibility he didn't.

She wrote her letter of resignation and left it on the desk in his office. In the guest suite, where they'd both been sleeping, she packed up everything she'd need for the next few weeks and lugged it out to her car. Then, she left a second note on the bed asking him to send anything she'd left behind to her parents' address in Chicago.

You have my number, she added, because maybe she did cling to hope after all, and she wanted him to know he was free to call.

At eight o'clock in the morning, when he still hadn't returned, she got in her car and drove to Forsyth, the next town over from Grand, and booked a room in a hotel so she could get a few hours of sleep. She didn't dare drive any farther in this semi-comatose state.

She called her mother to let her know when to expect her.

"Hi," she said, as cheerfully as she could. She didn't want

her parents to worry. She was fine. "I'm tired of Montana. I miss Chicago. I miss you. I have all the research notes I need for my dissertation, so I quit my job and I'll be home in a few days."

She chatted for a bit, about what she had no idea, then curled up in a ball on the bed and refused to think about what she was leaving behind. She'd spent years advocating for victims who didn't have any voice.

What other decision could she possibly have made and still live with herself?

Chapter Fourteen

Ryan

RYAN STARED STUPIDLY, first at the note in his hand, then the open bedroom closet door, and finally, the scattered feminine belongings. A pink scarf. A pair of impractically high heels. A long red hair snagged on one of his discarded socks that had missed the laundry basket in the corner.

His tired brain was running on fumes so the information took longer to process.

Elizabeth was gone.

The overwhelming sense of loss knocked the floor from beneath him and he had to sit down. The bed protested his assault on its box spring by shying beneath him. He hadn't experienced such a catastrophic event in his life since he'd been seven years old.

He crumpled the note. He must have begun breathing again because he was conscious. Perhaps her leaving was for the best. He'd driven around all night and hadn't come up with a solution that might work for them both.

He'd have the ranch's lawyer draw up an agreement for financial support. She didn't need his money—she likely wouldn't want it—but this whole mess was as much his fault as hers. More so, because he'd been aware of the stakes and she wasn't. She didn't understand that he'd dodged turning into another Giaco only because he'd seen what his grandfather had done to his father.

Thank God for the ranch, his friends, and Montana. They all kept him human.

The sun was up. Fingers of light clawed a path through the bedroom, grabbing at the walls and the floor. He didn't have the luxury to sit here, wishing he could crawl into bed and wake up with Elizabeth beside him, and discover the past sixteen hours had been a bad dream. She was gone and he had a ranch to run.

He didn't know what to do about the first, but the second was easy.

He went to work.

He was in the machine shed a week later, checking over the equipment so he could prioritize repairs, when Dallas's voice crackled over the hand-held radio on one of the roughly hewn wooden shelves.

"Dan and I are taking you to Lou's for supper. Doctor's orders. You have half an hour to shower and get ready to go." The set crackled. "Dan says the shower was ordered by the Department of Health and Human Services."

Lou's Pub was a favorite local hangout. The friends often

ate there, and played a few games of darts, although since Dallas and Hannah had gotten so close, they'd begun spending evenings at Hannah's taproom instead.

Ryan set his wrench down. The slight stir in the air gave his nose a clue as to why a shower had been demanded. He went off to comply.

A few minutes before seven, the men walked into Lou's. The inside smelled of stale beer and hot grease. Ryan's empty stomach rejoiced. He hadn't been paying a whole lot of attention to meals the past week, and today, he'd missed lunch.

They chose a table near the back.

"You've been working too hard," Dan said once they'd placed their orders. "You need to slow down."

Dan was wrong. He slept better at night when he was worn out and too tired to think.

"You've been doing this ever since Elizabeth left," Dallas butted in, adding his unwanted opinion. He was one of those people who genuinely cared about others and friendly concern wafted off of him now. From anyone else, Ryan would find it enraging. "Want to talk about it?"

"Nothing to talk about," Ryan said.

He wasn't about to be dragged into a discussion about Elizabeth, which was where this was headed. He'd destroyed any possibilities for reconciliation there. Besides, she might have better luck raising the ticking time bomb she carried if he stayed out of her way. She knew what a sociopath was, so she had that advantage.

"I beg to differ." Dan played with his fork, a sure sign he was troubled. "We've had a number of people ask us to speak with you on their behalf. Let's start with Miles. He has issues over the rodeo." He cleared his throat. "I'm trying to find a kind way to say this… You're in his way."

"The rodeo was my idea," Ryan said.

"Yes, it was your brainchild. But you hired Miles to take charge. You have to allow him to make his own decisions. If you don't, he'll leave. There are plenty of other circuit towns that would gladly hire him away. Besides"—now Dan looked downright uneasy—"Grand's chamber of commerce prefers working with him. It seems you can be—and I quote—'a real pain in the ass.'"

Ryan didn't give a damn about the chamber of commerce's collective opinion of him, but felt he should protest for appearances' sake. "That's harsh."

"It's a valid assessment," Dallas said. "No offense." He was facing the door, and as he glanced past Ryan's shoulder, he blanched. "Uh-oh. Incoming. Don't look around. Maybe she won't see us."

Ryan didn't know who "she" was, but based on Dallas's reaction, he could take a wild guess. Could his life possibly get any worse?

He kicked his low, round-backed chair away from the squat wooden table. "Gotta go to the bathroom."

But he was too late.

"Gentlemen," Adriana Gallant said, far too pleasant and friendly for his peace of mind. A typical feline, she liked to toy with her prey. "How lucky to find you all in the same place. I have a few questions that require confirmation. Mind if I join you?" She didn't wait for their agreement, but took the spare seat at the table. "This won't take long."

Ryan sank into his chair. If the past thirteen months were any indication, she'd keep hounding them until one of them broke and she'd gotten her story. All he had to do was keep his mouth shut and let Dan, who'd been on the receiving end of one of her interviews before, do the talking. He knew the drill.

"Anything for a pretty lady," Dan said, all country charm. "Fire away."

"Is it true that Ian Palmeter was the presiding judge who let you all off with a warning after you stole a police car in college?"

"There was community service involved," Dan said.

"Rumor has it that the judge left the three of you over four billion dollars as well as the Endeavour Ranch."

Uneasiness nestled into Ryan's chest. He wondered where she'd heard that particular story. The story was false. Except it was possible he might have led Dan and Dallas to believe it was true.

"You ever hear the saying, 'A rumor without a leg to stand on will get around some other way'?" Dan asked Adriana, oblivious to the disaster unfolding around him.

"Spreading stories with no basis in fact isn't news."

Big mistake, Dan. Calling the stories Adriana produced news was too great a stretch. No way would she buy into that.

Her gaze sharpened. "According to my sources, this particular rumor has quite a leg to support it. They say your money came from Giaco the 'Jackal' Cienetti's estate."

Ryan's heart skidded across his lungs before it braked to a halt. His blood sloshed around like the contents of a speeding oil truck approaching an unexpected red light. He'd told his friends a few vague bits and pieces about his background over the years. They'd guessed about witness protection. They'd suspected illegal connections.

They hadn't known his grandfather's name or that he was such a high-profile figure.

Dan donned his sheriff face. The one that went blank. The one that said he'd spotted the disaster too late and now damage control was the best he could hope for. The one that Adriana Gallant was about to ignore. "Never heard of him."

She tucked a sleek lock of dark hair behind her ear. "He was a Chicago mob boss. Stories have been circulating about his missing daughter and her husband and son for years. One suggests he had his son-in-law killed for skimming money. A new rumor surfaced shortly after he passed away. That one claims his daughter Angela and her son Giaco junior entered the witness protection program—or the witness security program, take your pick—right after Giaco senior had

Angela's husband murdered. It further claims that Angela died before her father did, meaning there was no more need for any witness protection, because Giaco junior was only seven when Angela took him out of Chicago." Her meaning, Ryan assumed, that as soon as his mother was out of the picture, anyone who had any knowledge of the case twenty-five years later would be free to talk. "He's of no interest to Giaco senior's remaining associates. But he was of great interest to his grandfather in the months before Giaco senior's death."

"I can't imagine what a rumor about a Chicago mob boss would have to do with us," Dan said. But Ryan could tell he was rattled.

Ryan was, too. His clenched fists trembled on his thighs under the table. In his head he was back in Chicago, watching the final moments of a father he'd loved very much.

"Giaco was a very rich man," Adriana continued, relentless. "It seems he made a lot of legitimate money through offshore investing. He left that money to his grandson. And since he only had one grandson that my sources are aware of, that would have to be Angela's son, Giaco junior."

"That's a great story," Dan said. "But it's got nothing to do with us. Food's here," he added cheerfully. Leila, Lou's pretty daughter, set a tray loaded with burgers and fries on the table. "Would you care to join us?" he asked Adriana as the plates were passed around. "Hey, Leila. Get Ms. Gallant whatever she likes and add it to our bill."

"No, thank you." Adriana consulted the screen on her phone. "I've got to get back to Billings to catch a late flight."

Their lack of cooperation didn't bother her in the least. No doubt she was used to it, given her line of work. Besides, she had her story. It didn't matter whether or not it was true. Plausibility won her the ratings.

After she left, and Leila disappeared into the kitchen, the table went silent. Dallas bit into his burger. Dan ate a few french fries. Ryan dug into his food, too.

They ate quietly until it became apparent that his friends were waiting on him.

"So," he said, since there was no time like the present, "you guys would probably like an explanation."

"LET ME SEE if I understand this correctly," Dallas said. "Judge Palmeter left us the ranch and enough money for land taxes for two years. The conditions are that if we sell the ranch or any parcels of land, all proceeds go to charity."

"Right," Ryan said.

He really had stayed in touch with Judge Palmeter over the years, as he'd said. He'd gone to Judge Palmeter for advice when his grandfather first made an appearance. It was the judge who'd convinced him to take the money rather than allow it to revert to a more dubious heir, then offered him the ranch as a means to control it.

"No offense, boy," the judge had said, *"but while your morals appear sound enough, your ethics can be questionable at times. You might want to think about how you can keep those ethics away from temptation."*

That was where Dan and Dallas and the conditions surrounding the inheritance came in. The judge had arranged it all for him because Ryan hadn't wanted the source of the money to affect Dan's career as a sheriff.

It was getting late. The pub's swinging kitchen doors flapped on their hinges as Leila and her father moved back and forth, filling the salt and pepper shakers and wiping down tables, sending a signal they were ready to close.

Dallas rubbed the back of his neck as if tormenting a crick. "But the rest of the money—billions of dollars—came from Giaco Cienetti. Your grandfather."

Ryan lifted his palms. "I didn't choose him for my grandfather. That was a cruel twist of fate. The money is legal, though. All of it. The judge made sure of that."

"You should have told us the whole story," Dan said. His lazy, good-humored exterior cracked, exposing the practical sheriff underneath—and the sheriff was unsurprised, meaning he'd had his suspicions.

"If I had, you wouldn't have accepted the money." Ryan had worried about that the most. It was no secret that neither one of his friends had slid easily into their new tax bracket.

"No," Dan said, direct, as usual. "We probably wouldn't.

But not because we ever thought it was dirty. You said from the start that it was a legal bequest and we chose to trust you. We do trust you. We would have turned it down because that money is rightfully yours, not ours."

"I didn't want it either. The judge talked me into it. He was also the one who said I should bring you both into it, too. He figured you'd help me stay honest."

"You're honest enough. Sort of. From a global perspective, and if we discount your uncanny ability to manipulate the truth. It's your trust issues that could use the most work," Dan said.

"You've made sure the money's being put to good use," Dallas, who never failed to see a bright side, threw in. "And if Adriana manages to piece the whole story together, that's what she'll find out—that the money supports three good causes—and it was all drawn up nice and legal by a retired judge who gave it his full support." He slapped Ryan on the back. "Well done, evil genius. We always said you should use your powers for good."

"We said, '*If only* he'd use his powers for good,'" Dan corrected him. "We never expected it to happen."

An enormous weight lifted off Ryan. He'd always dreaded what might happen if his friends found out where the money came from and his role in maneuvering them onto the ranch. He should have given them more credit.

"Which brings us back to our original reason for taking you out for dinner," Dallas added. "Since you're on a roll, you might as well tell us what went wrong with Elizabeth, too. We already know you're the one who screwed that relationship up."

"You don't know that for sure."

Dallas's right eyebrow vanished under a forelock of black curly hair. "Who here at the table told a four-billion-dollar lie and covered up the story of having a mafia grandpa?"

"Not me," Dan said, raising his hands in a warding-off gesture.

Ryan was too relieved that his friends hadn't demanded to be let out of the ranch and the money to take issue. "You guys are jealous because my life is so much more worldly."

"Sure. That's got to be it." Dan folded his arms and leaned on the table, getting cozy. "Spill. Does it have anything to do with Elizabeth being pregnant?"

"How did you know that?"

"Dallas told me."

That left Ryan speechless.

"Don't look at me like that," Dallas said hastily, seeing exactly where Ryan's thoughts went. "No, I did not play doctor with her. We bumped into each other in the lounge and the pregnancy tests fell out of the bag." He looked thoughtful. "That's kind of ironic, don't you think? Since the cat's out of the bag too?"

They knew she was pregnant. There seemed little reason to keep the rest of the story a secret from them, although this secret was unlikely to make him feel as good to unload. "I asked her to have an abortion."

"*Du-u-u-de*," Dallas said. His face shone with reproof. "That's not cool."

Dan, for his part, usually liked to get all the facts straight before he passed judgment. If he disapproved of any of this, he wasn't letting on yet. "What did she say to that?"

"She said it's her body and she's the only person who gets to make that decision."

"She's right," Dallas said.

"It gets worse." Ryan might as well unload everything. "I told her it's either the baby or me."

Dallas went back to worrying the crick in his neck. "Way to set yourself up for rejection. Need me to explain pregnancy hormones to you?"

"No thanks, I got to see them in action firsthand."

"I bet." Dan shook his head. "You're going to have to work extra hard to fix this one, my moronic friend."

"It can't be fixed."

"Yes, it can. Elizabeth is a lot more sympathetic toward human nature and its many flaws than you are by far. But you'll have to admit a few things about yourself, first."

"I'm a selfish ass. I know it." He'd heard it from her, although not in quite such explicit terms.

"Well, yeah. But that's not what I'm talking about. You have to start trusting the people you're closest to. That means trusting we know what's best for you when it's obvious you don't have a clue," Dan said.

"Do you trust us?" Dallas asked, getting in on the *kick Ryan while he's down* action that Ryan was trying hard not to resent. But his friends were perfectly serious, and the truth was, he did trust them. He also trusted Elizabeth.

He was the one with the problem.

"I trust you."

"Okay, then." Dan made himself comfortable, which guaranteed Ryan was about to experience the exact opposite effect. "Here's the first harsh truth you need to hear. Elizabeth came to you because she believed you had a right to know you're going to be a father. She likely expected a small amount of emotional support. In return, you issued her an ultimatum that went against everything she believes in. Then, when she didn't make the choice you wanted—and you'd better believe it's her choice—you let her walk away. You've got to stop testing your friends and start trusting us more. You didn't give Dallie and me a choice about the money and you didn't give Elizabeth any real choices, either. Will you man up and be a father, at least?"

"No." He was adamant about that.

His friends stared at him in disbelief.

"My mother spent her whole life doing her best to make sure I didn't turn out like her father. I'm not going to raise another Giaco Cienetti, either."

"Try raising another Ryan O'Connell," Dallas said, shrugging his shoulders, as if the solution were really that simple. "Your mother managed to do it mostly right. I have faith in Elizabeth, too. If that's all you're worried about—that you'll end up with a Giaco junior—she's the perfect person to see that doesn't happen."

"Do you love her?" Dan interrupted.

More than anything. He'd missed her every second of every day. He'd never regretted anything more than letting her leave, especially with so many unresolved issues between them. The condom calamity was a poor second. He had to work himself into a coma to get any sleep.

He couldn't admit any of that though. If he started unloading those feelings, he'd lose what little control of himself he had left. "What kind of question is that?"

Relentless interrogation was one of Dan's strengths. "A fair one. Here's the second harsh truth. You're going to be a father, whether you like it or not. Elizabeth is going to raise this baby, with or without you. She's a beautiful, smart, practical woman. She's got her own money and she doesn't need you. Sooner or later, she's going to find someone who'll be more than happy to be a father to her baby. Right now, you have a say in who that father will be. Once Elizabeth finds someone else, you'll have no say at all. Is that what you want?"

God, no.

He'd been so focused on her having a baby he didn't want that he hadn't considered the possibility she might someday find another man. One more thought to keep him sleepless at night.

"You can be a real bastard," he said to Dan.

"I take it you're starting to get what you stand to lose."

"Yeah. I do." And it scared him, because if—when—she found someone else, there'd be no getting her back.

It might be too late for him already.

"I always figured you and Hannah would be the first to have kids," Dan said to Dallas, while Ryan quietly hyperventilated in silence.

"We might have, if only I'd shown Ryan how to use those condoms I gave him," Dallas replied. "In my defense, I usually only have to give that demonstration to teenagers."

"I know how to use a condom," Ryan said, once the dizziness passed—as if that was what was important right now. He had to find some way to make this right.

The solution he'd searched for the night she'd told him she was pregnant suddenly presented itself with a clarity that lit up the dark pub. He might not be able to love any child he'd helped spawn, but he had no trouble at all loving Elizabeth. He couldn't imagine a woman more perfect.

He'd ask her to marry him and pray she said yes. They'd take the future one step at a time. How long might it take for a child's sociopathic tendencies to emerge, anyway? Eight years? Ten? Maybe twelve?

Leila headed toward them, their bill in her hand—another, more direct, hint that the pub was ready to close.

Dallas reached for his wallet. "I'll get it."

"Why are you sitting here?" Dan demanded of Ryan. "Shouldn't you be on your way to Chicago by now?"

223

Chapter Fifteen

Elizabeth

"WE'LL TURN YOUR closet into a nursery and open up the bedroom next to yours for you to use as an office and additional storage," Elizabeth's mother announced. "We can pick out baby furniture whenever you're ready."

The Bensons were having breakfast in the sunroom off the kitchen while planning their day. Gusts of rain lashed the glass panels. Flashes of lightning firebombed the bleak sky. Rumbles of thunder left the walls quaking. Elizabeth loved a good storm. Outside, chaos reigned. Inside, the sunroom was tidy and cozy and safe.

She dusted toast crumbs off her fingers and onto the clear crystal plate and considered the significance of her mother's words. The bedroom next to hers had once been Marianne's. It wasn't a shrine, all of her sister's belongings had been removed and the furniture replaced, but neither had it been occupied since her death. That her mother planned on letting it go was a major step forward and so

Elizabeth picked her answer with care.

"My being here is only temporary," she reminded her gently.

Meredith Benson patted her daughter's hand. The faraway cast to her eyes suggested she was sorting through color palettes, not listening. "Of course, sweetheart. We know that. But there's no harm in us making room for you when you and the baby stay over on holidays, is there?"

Absolutely no harm at all. Elizabeth hadn't seen her parents this happy or excited or animated in years and seeing it now warmed her heart.

"Of course not. Thank you for thinking of it," she said.

They'd been wonderful ever since she broke the news that they were going to be grandparents. Their enthusiasm hadn't spilled over into helping her find a place of her own, but she'd already called her father's office and his executive assistant was on it.

They hadn't been pleased when they'd learned who the baby's father was, though. She'd had to do a lot of fast talking to keep Theo Benson from boarding the next flight to Montana in order to *set Ryan O'Connell straight as to what a man's responsibilities are.* She didn't want her father to hate him, but sharing his confidences wasn't her right, so she'd settled on, *"It's complicated,"* as an explanation for where their relationship stood at the moment.

"The hell it's complicated," her father fired back. *"The sonofabitch was your boss."*

The ring of the doorbell cut through the roar of the storm, startling Elizabeth out of her thoughts.

Her father set his napkin down and started to rise. "Who could that be on a morning like this? Anyone expecting a delivery?"

"I'll get it," she said, waving him into his chair. "Finish your breakfast. I'm done with mine." Dry toast was still the best she could manage.

The doorbell pealed again, escalating to a persistent buzz as its assailant leaned into it. Whoever it was, they were impatient. A seed of hope took root in her chest.

She quickened her steps and hurried through the foyer. When she answered the door, the seed sprouted roots. Her heart tripped over its own feet in excitement.

Ryan's presence in the portico was heralded by a deep roll of thunder and accompanying flash of the sky. Rain dripped from the brim of his hat. He had on the same long, oilskin duster he wore herding cattle, and he'd paired it with a Stetson, denim jeans, and a scuffed pair of cowboy boots— not an outfit one saw too many men wearing on the streets of Chicago. He couldn't scream *cowboy* with a bullhorn any louder.

Dark eyes soaked up every detail of her appearance in return, from the messy bun and lack of makeup, right down to the black sweatshirt and leggings and felt slippers. His mouth clenched at the corners.

"And you thought a little Montana downpour was an

extreme weather event," he said, typically foregoing any displays of affection.

But she saw what he held bottled up in his eyes.

"I'm so happy to see you," she began, but his eyes had drifted over her head to the far worse dark force of nature looming behind her.

"You must be Ryan O'Connell." Her father's tone was as cold and unwelcoming as she'd ever heard it. "Come in."

Unfortunately, Ryan managed to channel his grandfather at the worst possible time. "I'd prefer to speak with Elizabeth alone," he said, dismissing her father, a catastrophic mistake if he'd come here to make peace. *Great going, Heathcliff.* "Come for a drive with me," he said to her.

No one dismissed Theo Benson, particularly in his own house. The storm had nothing on what was about to occur. "While I'd prefer you not speak to my daughter at all, I accept that you're the father of her child and you have legal rights." *Should you ever dare try to enforce them*, his caustic tone added, and wasn't this going well. "Let's take this opportunity to get a custody agreement on paper before the baby is born. *Come in.*"

"I'll sign anything she wants. First, I'd like to speak to her in private." Ryan didn't take his eyes off Elizabeth. "Come with me," he said softly.

"The streets are a mess." Her father stared pointedly at the pellets of rain bouncing a foot off the walkway. "The safety of my daughter and grandchild might not mean much to you, but they're of the utmost importance to her mother and me."

"That's unfair," Elizabeth said, frowning at him.

"I'll take care of her." Ryan's attention reverted to her, the hardness in his eyes cracking. "Please."

Hope bounced around in her chest. She'd half-expected a letter from his lawyer, outlining his obligations in impartial detail. Instead, he'd come here, himself.

"It's okay, Dad. I'll get my coat."

Rain fell in buckets from the sky and gushed into storm drains on the street. Wind whipped it against their backs. Ryan braced one arm behind her and held her hand with the other, shielding her from the elements on the short walk to the car. If her father was watching this display of gentlemanly behavior, he'd be so impressed.

"You drove all the way from Grand? Why not fly?" she asked once Ryan had positioned himself behind the wheel. He didn't seem to notice or care that they dripped water all over the AMG's custom interior. Rain pounded the windshield.

"I think best when I drive."

And it was obvious he had a lot on his mind, because he'd driven quite a distance.

After fifteen minutes of silence, and they'd turned off the I-90 and onto the I-290, it became obvious that sharing his thoughts wasn't part of his plan. Some questions might be in order.

"Are you kidnapping me?" she asked.

The windshield wipers tapped left, then right. The line of his jaw shifted in acknowledgment of her pitiful attempt at a joke. "Your father took a picture of my car and the license plate as we were pulling away, so it's safe to say that my kidnapping plot has been thwarted."

"I've told you how protective he can be. And I'm pretty sure you didn't make a favorable impression on him."

The right side of Ryan's cheek kicked up a full inch. When he cast his gaze sideways at her, she saw he was smiling. "I figured it was too late for that anyway, so decided I'd expend my efforts on the person who matters most."

That smile stole her breath. She was so *easy* when he went all Black Bart on her. Where was her pride?

She went back to staring through her window at the streets passing by. The car was quiet for a few moments more. She folded her hands on her belly. Sadness tightened her chest. Ryan wouldn't be interested in the little changes in her body that fascinated her so much.

"Where are we going?" she asked.

"You'll have to wait and see."

So much for that conversational thread. She tried again. "How are the boys?"

"As obnoxious as ever. Ace has Jonas in mental health counseling until he's ready to open up about his sexual orientation."

"That's reasonable. He hasn't come to terms with it."

She gave up trying to make small talk after that and allowed him to concentrate on traffic while his GPS gave him directions.

They took an exit into an upscale neighborhood about ten minutes outside the city limits. He pulled curbside in front of a brick-and-stone, Spanish-style mansion. The mansion was surrounded by well-established, decades-old trees on a large corner lot. Shrubs and flower beds suggested the gardens would be spectacular whenever someone took them in hand. A concrete path meandered from a wrought iron gate to the front door.

"This is where I lived as a little kid," he said.

He sounded matter-of-fact about it, but the way his white-knuckled fingers strangled the life from the steering wheel suggested he had a whole lot of issues swirling around in his head. He'd decided to face his childhood trauma and she could only imagine how hard this must be. He'd been *seven years old*.

She tossed pride aside and reached for his hand. "I'm so sorry."

He transferred his chokehold to her fingers, but she didn't complain. He was too lost in his head and she didn't want to intrude. His whole attention was transfixed by the house.

He pointed to the second level. "See that third window, to the right of the front door? That was my bedroom. It had race cars on the walls. My dad painted them himself."

One more reason for him to like cars and speed—they connected him to his father.

"He was a great dad," Ryan continued. "A lot of happy memories were made in this house, not just the bad ones. But let me paint a more complete family picture for you. Giaco approached me a few months before he passed away. Turns out he'd known where we were all along. He offered me money if I'd move back to Chicago and take on his name again. I'm the last of his line and he didn't want the name to die with him. I told him what he could do with his name and his money and figured that would be that, but he left the money to me anyway. It came from legitimate holdings he used to keep him respectable, in case you're wondering."

"I wasn't wondering." Because she knew him. He would have burned every dishonest dollar.

She regretted ever thinking of him as cold, because it only reinforced how he viewed himself. He was definitely tormented—she'd seen it from the first and known it would never be easy to live with—but he'd done so much to rise above what he perceived as his failings. He had a mind-boggling amount of inner strength. This would be the luckiest child alive to have him for a father.

He wasn't quite ready to hear that about himself, though.

"Why did you take the money if you didn't want it?" she asked.

"Because my mother missed having it from the day she

walked through the door. She'd been born rich and she didn't know how to be poor, although she tried her best for my sake. And because there's a part of me that's driven by money. I like to make it work for me. I figured I'd take it and I'd use it to do something good—sort of an in-your-face to the Jackal and everything he stood for. A judge I used to know drew up agreements that tied it up so the bulk of it could only be spent for philanthropic purposes. He didn't think I should be tempted." He smiled thinly. "That's where Dan and Dallie come in. They make sure the money gets spent where it's supposed to go. The ranch provides the bulk of our personal incomes—and believe me, there isn't much profit coming out of a ranch."

She touched the sleeve of his coat. "For what it's worth, I don't see a thing wrong with you taking the money and making it work for you. And your mother must have been an amazing woman. Giaco Cienetti's daughter, knowing what he was capable of, turned her back on him and did what was best for her son."

"If I'd grown up under my grandfather's influence, I'd be sitting exactly where he was, right now."

"Maybe. Maybe not. You don't know that for sure. All I know is that I fell in love with the man you are, not some hypothetical person you might have become."

He closed his eyes for a second. His tension level visibly dropped, leaving him looking about a thousand times more vulnerable than she'd ever seen him.

He opened his eyes. "I love you, Elizabeth. I knew you'd turn my whole life upside down the moment you showed up for your job interview, and you did. But I never intended to ruin yours. This past week has been hell." A wry smile twisted his mouth. "Dan and Dallas begged me to come get you—right after Dallas gave me a lecture on a woman's right to autonomy over her body." The smile disappeared. "I love you so much I'll do anything for you, if you'll only come back to Grand with me—as long as you understand I can't love this baby. I'll be a terrible father. I'm sorry."

She didn't believe for one second that a man who cared as much about troubled teens as he did was incapable of loving his own child, but she also didn't expect miracles to happen overnight, and there was no reason to push him. He'd figure it out on his own, in his own time and his own way.

She did understand that the coming months were going to be hard on them both. They had a lot to work through. He wouldn't want to feel the baby's movements or go to prenatal checkups with her, so she'd pretty much have to go it alone, but the end result would be worth it. He hadn't wanted to love her any more than he'd wanted a baby—and yet he did love her.

He'd come for her.

Her heart broke into song. "Why don't you work on winning over my parents first—since you've made such a stellar first impression on them—and worry about what kind of father you'll be when it happens?"

"Win over your parents? What other impossible tasks do I have to complete? This might turn into a kidnapping, after all." He took one last, long look at the house, then started the car. "I can do one thing right for this baby, at least. I'll make sure it's born in Montana, not here." He turned to her. She read the raw plea on his face. Heard it in the rasp of his voice. "Can you forgive me?"

"I can forgive you anything, Heathcliff."

She itched to be in his arms. The confined space meant it was one more thing she'd have to wait for. Instead, she cupped his cheeks and drew his face closer to hers so that she could kiss him and wipe away any remaining doubts he might have. Happiness wiped away any lingering doubts of her own.

Ryan always did what was right—when he was ready.

"Let's go talk to my parents," she said. "Then, take me home to Montana."

Epilogue

Ryan

THE DELIVERY ROOM had roughly twenty people in it—or that was how it appeared. Ryan was too stressed out to conduct an accurate count. He concentrated on staying as close to his wife's side as he could without getting in anyone's way.

Another contraction contorted her small frame and her back arched in a bow. She squeezed his hand, hard, and he winced—in sympathy, not pain. Although, if he could take it on for her, he'd gladly switch places. She'd been in labor for seventeen hours and he didn't think his nerves could take it much longer. Twice now, a nurse had suggested he take a break in the waiting room—he suspected because his demands they see to Elizabeth's comfort might be out of line—but her parents were in the waiting room too, and Theo Benson made no effort to hide his continued dislike for his new son-in-law.

Ryan got it. He didn't think he was good enough for Elizabeth, either. He certainly wasn't much good to her right now.

Yet one more gowned and masked medical professional entered the room. A woman. As she approached Elizabeth, two workers moved out of her way. At last. A doctor.

The doctor did a quick examination. "She's crowning," she said with satisfaction. Her eyes smiled at Ryan over her mask. "You're about to find out if you have a son or a daughter, Dad."

Dad.

Oh, my God.

Ryan felt faint. He wasn't ready for this. He'd be a terrible father. He hadn't been able to work up any enthusiasm during the final months of Elizabeth's pregnancy. No matter how many times she tried to reassure him it was natural not to be excited before he had a baby to hold in his hands, he couldn't believe her. What if he didn't have it in him? What if he failed as a father and raised another Giaco Cienetti to unleash on the world?

Elizabeth cried out. Ryan winced.

"Push, Mom," the doctor ordered, her head bent between Elizabeth's shaking thighs and her hands busy doing things Ryan couldn't see. He was too preoccupied with his wife and how she was holding up.

"And… it's a girl!" the doctor announced. "You have a daughter."

A girl?

It took Ryan a few seconds to process the news. Never

once had it occurred to him that he might end up with a daughter. A little bubble of joy encompassed his heart. He abandoned Elizabeth without a second's hesitation, anxious for proof that the howling bundle the doctor cradled in her gloved hands was, indeed, a baby girl. "Are you sure?"

The room exploded with laughter.

"I'm rarely wrong at this stage," the doctor assured him, a smile in her voice.

The baby was whisked away before he could see for himself. He turned on the doctor. "What are they doing to her?" he demanded, going Giaco on them.

"We're weighing and measuring her, and generally making sure she's in good health," the doctor said. "It's all standard procedure. She's fine. You can hold her as soon as they've got her cleaned up and bundled."

Elizabeth reached for his hand. "Relax, Heathcliff," she murmured. Exhaustion rimmed her amber eyes. "They've got everything under control. Can someone let my parents know they have a granddaughter?"

Ryan clung to Elizabeth, but he couldn't take his eyes off his daughter. The wait was excruciating, although only a few minutes passed before one of the nurses laid the tiny, blanketed bundle in his shaking arms.

"We're going to wheel your wife to a recovery room so you can be alone as a family for a bit before we take your daughter off to the nursery for a few hours," someone said. "Mom needs to rest."

Moments later, they were alone. Ryan held the baby, refusing to give her up, even after the nurse gently suggested Elizabeth might like a turn. His daughter was red-faced and wrinkled, with a tiny, puckered mouth, and eyelids squeezed tightly shut. She was the most beautiful creature he'd ever seen—next to her mother, of course.

Elizabeth was watching him, a smile of pure pleasure on her face, although she could barely keep her eyes open.

"I'm sorry," Ryan said. "You can hold her. Just give me one more minute."

"Take as many as you'd like," Elizabeth said. "I held her for nine months. It's your turn now. All I want to do is go to sleep."

"I'm so relieved she's a girl," he whispered. He placed a soft, careful kiss on the tiny, wrinkled forehead.

"Girls can be sociopaths too, you know. But don't worry. She won't start off as an evil crime lord. She'll grow into the role. You'll have years to get used to the idea."

"You aren't helping."

Elizabeth laughed, although it was more of a tired smile accompanied by a puff of sweet air. "When I first met you, you delivered a newborn calf. All I could think about was how amazing it was that you'd brought this tiny new life into the world. It made you the sexiest man I'd ever met. But I have to say, there's nothing sexier than watching a beautiful man hold a new life he helped to create."

"If I didn't love you already, that statement right there

would have sealed the deal." He gazed down at the baby. "I'm pretty sure I'm going to love this little lady, too." In fact, he was almost positive he couldn't love her any more than he did at this moment. "What are we going to name her?"

"Sure. Now you want to talk about names," Elizabeth said, which made him feel guilty, even though she was teasing. He'd avoided the subject for weeks. He hadn't been able to get his head past all the worry, and yet, she'd been amazingly patient and understanding with him. He'd married a saint.

"I have a few suggestions, but I want to hear your thoughts on it, first," she added.

His thoughts were a mess. He struggled to collect them so that they'd make sense. "She's the first in the family to be born with the O'Connell name. She's also a first-generation Montanan. She deserves to have something original—all her own—to go with the other firsts. I don't want her to be touched by either of our pasts, so sorry, I don't want to name her after any family members. I want her name to represent the future. Okay. Those are my thoughts. Let's hear your suggestions."

"I suspected you might feel that way, and I took it into consideration. How about Naomi Mathilda?" Elizabeth said. She could barely keep her eyes open. "Naomi means sweetness, beauty, and gentleness. And Mathilda means strength—because she's going to have to be tough to grow up on the Endeavour Ranch."

"Clever. You managed to name her after yourself." He kissed her, mindful of the tiny bundle he held. "Naomi Mathilda O'Connell it is. The Endeavour won't know what hit it. Get your rest, beautiful. As soon as we get the okay, I'm taking you both home."

The End

Don't miss the next book in the Grand, Montana series, *The Cowboy's Christmas Baby*!

Join Tule Publishing's newsletter for more great reads and weekly deals!

If you enjoyed *The Montana Rancher,*
you'll love the next book in…

The Grand, Montana series

Book 1: *The Montana Sheriff*

Book 2: *The Montana Doctor*

Book 3: *The Montana Rancher*

Book 4: *The Cowboy's Christmas Baby*
Coming in October 2022

Available now at your favorite online retailer!

More books by Paula Altenburg

The Montana McGregor Brothers series

Book 1: *The Rancher Takes a Family*

Book 2: *The Rancher's Secret Love*

Book 3: *The Rancher's Proposal*

A Sweetheart Brand series

Book 1: *Her Montana Brand*

Book 2: *The Cowboy's Brand*

Book 3: *Branded by the Cowboy*

Available now at your favorite online retailer!

About the Author

USA Today Bestselling Author Paula Altenburg lives in rural Nova Scotia, Canada with her husband and two sons. A former aviation and aerospace professional, Paula now writes contemporary romance and fantasy with romantic elements.

Thank you for reading

The Montana Rancher

If you enjoyed this book, you can find more from all our great authors at TulePublishing.com, or from your favorite online retailer.

TULE
PUBLISHING